Ephphatha
Catholic Fiction for Modern Times

Philip J Martin

Full Quiver Publishing
Pakenham, ON

Published by Full Quiver Publishing, PO Box 244, Pakenham, ON K0A2X0, a Division of Innate Productions.

For Jennifer, whom I love

Acknowledgments

It has taken many years to write and compile these stories, and one person has been more instrumental in its completion more than any other. Jennifer, thank you for being a wonderful support to my endeavors over the years, particularly this one. Thank you for recognizing this and other creative endeavors as an outlet for this introvert!

For giving me and my writing its initial verification, I must thank Peter Mongeau of Tuscany Press for recognizing *The Laying on of Hands* and *The Grove* as stories worthy of public recognition. Also, thank you to Jeanne Lyet Gassman for working with me in editing *The Laying on of Hands*. Special thanks to Dan Johnson, Jack McAleer, Jamie McAleer and all at 4PM Media for allowing me the opportunity to work on the *Sign of Contradiction* project. And to my parents, James and Julie Martin, thank you for putting me through an exceptional education and showing me the meaning of hard work. For all others who have ever given feedback or made positive comments on any of my stories and articles, know of my appreciation.

Table of Contents

The Laying on of Hands

The merciless Alabama sunshine beat down on the boys as they tramped through the shallow water. Ethan's wet legs and a slight breeze chilled him. He lengthened his strides and stalked like a thief to keep the splashing to a minimum. Up ahead, his older brother Wiley gripped a rusty hatchet by its worn rubber handle. He halted abruptly every now and then to peer left and right while his free hand shaded his eyes like the baseball cap his father never bought him. Ethan had spotted the tool nearly a week ago in the tall grass that grew along the right side of the ditch. He claimed it as his own, but after a bit of bickering, reluctantly submitted ownership of the small ax to his sibling. The humidity had dulled the blade and coated it with rust. Their father's amateur attempt to sharpen it left the tip bent and the cast iron further scratched and weakened.

Ethan's weapon, a thick limb cut from a mature crepe myrtle, doubled as a walking stick. Stopping to glance over his shoulder at Lee, a neighborhood friend who often accompanied them on these adventures, Ethan wondered if damp legs were a good enough excuse to turn back and go home.

"How many snakes've you killed, Lee?" Ethan asked.

Lee thought for a moment before saying, "In my life? A few dozen. But this summer, just a couple, 'cause of my job."

Ethan would have given anything for a job, even if it paid nothing. Little money meant little to do. With both parents mostly absent, he and Wiley were free to hunt or do as they pleased for the summer. This meant that, for all intents and purposes, Wiley was in charge.

"Hurry up!" Wiley yelled like a commanding officer from some distance ahead. Wiley's shirt was tied around his waist and bounced as he walked. His bony shoulders glowed red like coals with sunburn. At thirteen and two years older, Wiley had a natural height and speed advantage over his eleven-year-old brother, and his legs were unusually long and thin, especially relative to the short, fat ones of Ethan. The younger, however, had been endowed with a bit of a talent when it came to music and had even taught himself to play a tune from Sunday school. If his father walked in, however, he would slam the lid over the keys and jump up from the bench. The piano was for little girls getting ready for recitals.

Is piano for girls?" he had asked his mother. His head lay in her lap, and as she scratched his back with long fingernails, Ethan knew he could ask or tell her anything. Still in her nurse's scrubs, she hummed Ethan's song while she reclined her head on a maroon pillow. Heaped ashes across the room in the fireplace from the preceding winter were a reminder of the cycles of the seasons. The simple wooden mantle above was adorned with a crucifix and a whiskey decanter in the shape of Paul Bunyan.

No," she slowly replied as if her answer were a part of the hymn. After seeing the song to its final note, she continued, "No, no, no. Do not listen to your father when he comes home in a silly mood or tired or upset after a long day of job interviews."

He's not silly, Mama, and he ain't tired either. Wiley told me he's drunk. He said it's when you drink too much whiskey."

Her nails dug a little deeper into his skin. "It doesn't matter how he walks through the door, sweetie," his mother whispered. "Just don't listen to him when he comes home like that. You listen to me, honey. Your father and your brother may be older than you, but that doesn't mean they know any better than you about right from wrong."

✠

At the roar of thunder, Wiley and Lee quickened their steps. As their bare feet struck the water, frightened tadpoles scattered like fireworks. The thick brown cowlick on the top of Wiley's head bobbed up and down and his scrawny arms swung like pendulums.

"Why are you in such a hurry?" Ethan called across the splashes.

We gotta get one before it rains," Wiley replied. "We gotta make it to where we did last week when Mama called us in, so just keep up!"

By the time the leaders began to slow, Ethan was a full thirty yards behind. The ditch had widened and the concrete walls had risen impregnable above them on either side. Weeds and dirt choked the flow of water. Wiley stalked about more like an egret than a human as they made their way along the islands of thick grass.

It seemed to Ethan that as his fear grew, so did Wiley's anticipation. "Remember," Lee called out, "they're more scared of you than you are of them."

This brought Ethan little comfort, yet like a blind man, he tapped at patches of vegetation with the stick before stepping near them. "Wiley," he pleaded, "I'm hungry; let's go back and see if we can meet Mama for lunch. Besides, it's about to rain, and this grass is too tall to even—"

Right there! There!" interrupted Wiley. "Pin it! Pin it! There against the wall! It's getting away! Quick, before it gets into a hole! Pin it!"

Out of fear of his brother's retribution, Ethan leapt twice toward the dark brown moccasin as it slithered past. He thrust the wood downward into the back of the serpent just below the neck and put his weight into it. Wiley followed and bent low over the foe.

Whack! The sound split open the thick, humid air like a coconut. Ethan lifted the rod and watched with the others as the undulating body drifted downstream after its own venomous head.

Wiping his moist brow with the back of the hand that held the hatchet, Wiley gloried in the kill. "The less poisonous snakes, the better," he said as if the safety of the community were his primary concern. His voice had grown deeper in recent months.

Ethan didn't respond. The snake's rippled path led his eyes down the ditch about fifty yards. The glare that reflected off of the water was sharp like flint, but when he squinted, he could make out a large hole like a mouth that opened up in the steep wall. Ethan stepped towards it with timidity, followed shortly thereafter by Wiley.

The hole was a tunnel with an inch of stagnant water, like a tongue resting on the bottom. Measuring nearly five feet in diameter, it was barely large enough to fit a slumped Ethan or a crouching Wiley. A tiny light radiated from the far end. Whether that light was ten feet or one mile away was beyond their experience to determine. Even their breath seemed to echo as they leaned in and out, one after the other.

"Imagine the size of the water moccasins in there!" exclaimed the elder brother.

"I'm not going in there!" Ethan insisted.

"You're right," Wiley responded, seemingly ignorant of his brother's tone, "let's get a couple of flashlights and come back tomorrow."

"I can't tomorrow 'cause I have to help my dad cut the grass," Lee said. He looked with doubt at the tunnel and shook his head. "Too narrow for me anyway."

"I said I'm not going in there, period," Ethan added.

"Oh, yes, we are! Don't tell me you're scared again! You scared?"

"No, I—"

"Afraid you're gonna get bit?"

"No, course not," lied Ethan. "I bet I can get a snake outta there. I just don't wanna squat down for that long to find one. Probably ain't one in there anyhow. Snakes like the sun. I know 'cause I killed one laid out in the sun."

"It's just you need to practice on that queer piano, that's it."

"Stop, no, that's not—"

"I've heard you and seen you sitting there slumped with your damn eyes closed, playing the same God-awful tune over and over and over and over." Wiley crouched on an invisible bench and dropped the hatchet to impersonate the strokes of an amateur pianist.

"Shut up, Wiley! And Mama says don't cuss 'cause—"

"And then Dad comes in drunk and tells you to make yourself useful like Mama. You know what Dad told me?"

Ethan looked down at the water. Mention of his father was a trump card because, unlike Wiley, he felt he barely knew the man.

"What?" whimpered Ethan out of genuine curiosity.

"He told me I'm a *man*," replied Wiley as he bent to retrieve the hatchet. He shot up straight, uncoiling like a whip, his ax in hand, with as much height and bravado as he could muster. "He told me I'm old enough to be a man and stay up late and tell Mama what to do and what I need and not the other way around. He said it was time for my first drink and gave me some of his whiskey in one of those tiny glasses. He said I should kill all the snakes I want and make you help me to get the girl out of you. He said he was proud of me 'cause I don't sit at the piano in a dress and waste my time playing high-pitched notes over and over."

Ethan felt his cheeks redden, and he dug his burning fingertips, the nails chewed to the quick, into the rough wood of the staff.

Wiley continued, "I told him about how you hate coming with me down in here, and he laughed and laughed and said that was typical."

"Shut up!" Ethan squeaked. "Shut up! I'm a man, too. He just ain't told me yet, that's all."

Keeling over in laughter, Wiley shook his head from side to side as if he were polishing the hatchet with his nose.

"I'll be in that tunnel before you!" Ethan threatened. "You'll see! You can't even fit. You're too tall! I'll get a snake by myself. I did it before. I don't need you."

Ethan turned around towards their home, fighting back tears as he raced past Lee. It was his tunnel. He had discovered it. He ought to have the right to declare it his. Wiley's cackling laughter rang in Ethan's ears, and he lifted his thumb to his mouth and ripped off the nail with his teeth.

"You'll never go in there!" Wiley yelled with hands cupped around his mouth. "You're a boy. I'm a man, dammit! Typical! You'll never go in 'cause you're scared to death! Typical!"

The speed with which he hiked burned Ethan's underworked calves. The memory of Wiley's incessant yelling pestered him like a horsefly with every step until he reached the place where the ditch met his backyard. Grass, untrimmed for years, snuck underneath the aging chain link fence that bordered their property and caressed down the gray wall like tangled vines. Ethan made his way through the backyard with haste, tossing his staff behind an azalea before wiping his brow as he crossed the threshold. The large gray tiles of the kitchen were cool against his bare feet. Pinned beneath a rooster-shaped salt shaker lay a note:

Boys, I'll be home around 3:30. For lunch, there s leftover casserole in the fridge. Put your plates (please!) in the dishwasher when finished. Love, Mom.

After a quick look around, it was clear his father was not home. Ethan, no longer hungry, started towards his bedroom but stopped short and turned into the family room. He spied his father's liquor cabinet and bent low. After prying the doors apart, Ethan reached with sweaty hands for one of the whiskey bottles, twisted off the top, sniffed, and then jerked his face away in horror from the fumes. For a moment, he paused when an image of his mother flashed across his mind like the glare of a passing car. On the other hand, if he wanted to be a man, he had to. Holding his nose, he slowly tilted back his head and sucked the mouth of the bottle like a straw.

Its golden contents rolled over his tongue and down his open throat, burning him from the inside out. He tried not to cough and thought that if his father or Wiley could see him, they would laugh and say this was typical. Ethan screwed on the top as if it were hot, shoved the bottle back, slammed the doors shut, and ran away from the jangling glass across the yellow carpet and down the hall to the room he shared with Wiley. Pausing in the doorway, he leaned against the frame as his stomach cursed him.

Ethan pushed away from the door and dropped like a falling tree on top of the tangle of white sheets on his bed. As his wet shorts gripped his legs, a new hatred for the piano and the resolve to confront his father boiled to the surface. "To hell with it," he whispered as if his mother were listening from the next room. "To hell with all of it."

✠

The front door opened and closed, waking Ethan from a brief slumber. Sticky from the heat and sore from the damp pile of sheets digging into his ribs, Ethan got to his feet and tread down the hallway to the family room, where his father stood hunched over with his hands pressed firmly against one arm of the leather couch. The man was red in the face and breathing hard, sweating a bit as moist brown bangs dangled like tentacles from his forehead. He looked up at Ethan. "Make yourself useful and get me the small trash can from the bathroom," he mumbled.

Ethan obeyed, and after dumping a few empty toilet paper rolls onto the black-and-white tile floor, he brought the plastic bin to his father. The man dropped it and leaned now like a fugitive with both hands against the wall.

"I'm a man," Ethan uttered as deeply as he could. "I do things just like you and Wiley do."

His father chuckled and straightened and took two steps towards Ethan as his son took three steps backwards. The tall man halted and leaned over the couch before sitting down like dead weight with one palm pressed firmly against his lips. As he sank deeply into the soft leather, he swallowed. "What have you done that makes you think you're a man, huh? What the hell've you done that makes you think you're anything like me?"

"I kill snakes," replied the boy.

"No, you help your brother kill snakes sometimes. That ain't the same."

"I killed one once all by myself, a rat snake. It was laid out in the sun, in the morning, eating a toad. I threw a huge rock on top of it and crushed it. Wiley wasn't even there; he was—"

"Coward," interrupted the drunk man, "it weren't even poisonous, and you had to kill it with a rock! I'd expect nothing less from a piano-playing..." He paused to swallow. "From a piano-playing, sissy son. Your mama's raised you the complete opposite of what I'd have done. You wanna be like your brother? You wanna be like me? You gotta prove it, you—"

Ethan kicked the trash can out of his path and marched to the opposite side of the room to the antique piano his father sat facing. After releasing the safety locks on each of the wheels, he attempted to push and pull the instrument to the front door to be rid of it, but it was too heavy. His father laughed.

Sprinting outside, Ethan searched for one of his father's tools to use on the piano. When he turned the corner, a ray of sunlight reflected off of something in the yard and stabbed him in the eyes. Ethan tiptoed with one arm outstretched as if walking in total darkness until his gnawed fingers made contact with the object that lay heavy in the tall grass.

It was the hatchet, his brother's hatchet, though Wiley was nowhere to be seen. Ethan picked it up by the handle as if on a dare and returned to the family room, where he stared at the piano. It had to go. He struck the first leg clean, and the body of the instrument nearly crushed his foot as it slammed to the floor. The deep groan of the piano soaked into the walls as Ethan pounded the remaining legs and the wood panels. When he began to strike the ivory keys, the father yelled out, "Son, son, enough, get the trash can!"

Ethan grabbed the trash can and presented it to his father, who took it in his hands, held it to his mouth, and vomited.

The boy endured with a stoic persistence the thick stench and sound. Finally, his father set the can aside and combed his fingers through his greasy hair to reorient himself.

"Sit," he said, and he sighed a deep breath that caressed Ethan's face. Placing his hands on the top of Ethan's head, he asked, "You always gonna be there for me like this? On my side, always gonna do what I say?"

Ethan nodded.

"All right, son," whispered the father between wet lips, "you're a man." Sliding his oily palms down the sides of the boy's face, the father slapped him lightly on the cheek and fell over sideways, falling asleep as soon as his body hit the leather.

Ethan rose from the couch. The thick silence, broken now and then by a soft snore, enveloped him like a heavy blanket. He stretched and then smirked at the thought of Wiley's face when he told his brother that manhood now belonged to both of them. As he paced from room to room, his footsteps echoed. Everything was new. He looked up at the mantle. The crucifix seemed to reach higher to the ceiling, and Babe the Blue Ox laid bluer and more submissive beneath the right hand of his master.

He felt like Paul Bunyan, like he ought to order someone around, like he ought to be praised for something. If he went into his tunnel and killed a snake, maybe he would be the talk at school. Nail biting might become a trend. His father would teach him how to skin it. He would hang it in the room he shared with Wiley, above his own bed, and Wiley would see it every day.

Ethan found a red flashlight beneath the mess at the bottom of his closet. He jammed the hatchet he'd left in the living room through a belt loop and glided through the kitchen and out the back door, where a gentle breeze hit his face as if to push him back into the house. Two dogs barked incessantly somewhere far off. Ethan reached into the bushes to retrieve his staff, which he tucked under his arm as he strode to the ditch with a resolve he had never known.

The water splashed as Ethan made haste for the tunnel. He heard someone shouting his name. Wiley was following him. Ethan quickened his pace past the spot where they had killed the snake and arrived at the entrance to the tunnel.

When he leaned in, he could make out the bright spot at the other end, and as he switched on the flashlight, he looked to his right to see Wiley practically running through the water, followed by Lee. Ethan almost wished his brother had already caught up so that he could reverse the morning's routine when Wiley had shoved the staff into his hands and had chosen the hatchet for himself. Instead, Ethan squeezed into the tunnel and dropped his stick, as it was more a nuisance than an aid in the narrow hole, and pulled the hatchet from his belt.

The passage was slippery from the standing water and nearly silent, save for the occasional vehicle that passed overhead. Ethan's light was only strong enough to give him ten feet or so of clarity. The same algae that caused his feet to slip and slide every few steps must have also been the source of the dull odor that contributed to the awful, frightening aura of the place. Drinking more whiskey was preferable to the terror he felt now. Realizing the near impossibility of what he had set out to accomplish, Ethan stopped. He started to turn back when Wiley's voice reverberated through the darkness.

"Stop! Ethan! Stop! My snake is in there. Dammit! Give me back my hatchet, or I'll come in there and beat you. I swear it, I will!"

"I'm not going in there, Wiley. I'm too tall," came Lee's muffled voice.

"You're a coward then, too!" shouted Wiley. "Wait here!"

Wiley's flashlight was much brighter than Ethan's, and as he shined it down the tunnel, the beam hit Ethan in the face, temporarily blinding him. Ethan raised his hand in front of his face, blinking.

Wiley laughed. "Typical! You coming back? Scared, just like Dad says. You need me to hold your hand on the way out? Typical!"

Ethan swung back around and pushed deeper into the tunnel, tucking the hatchet under his arm so that he could steady himself on the curved wall. His anger had cloaked his fear, but now he shook like a leaf. Wiley was gaining on him and pitching insults forward like grenades.

Ethan froze in place and gasped. His light had fallen on the coiled body of a large moccasin with its cottonmouth agape and long fangs exposed. The bright white of its gums contrasted sharply with the dark body. Alert and defensive, its copper eyes seemed to jut out of the diamond head. A sharp hiss punctured the sloshing sound of Wiley's footsteps. Ethan faced the snake, equally alert, with his hatchet held out as a shield between them.

Wiley peered over the shoulder of his younger brother. "Gimme my hatchet," he ordered. "And here's your stick."

"No way, Wiley, I found it in the first place. It's mine." Ethan spoke softly, never taking his eyes off the snake. "Besides, Dad just told me I'm a man, too, so guess what? That means I'm keeping the damn thing for myself, and I can kill this snake by myself. I don't need you or your help. Go away!"

"You gave the hatchet to me," yelled Wiley with a renewed fury. "Now give it back!" As he said this, he dropped the staff and pushed Ethan to the side. Then Wiley reached across and gripped the hatchet by the handle. Ethan fell to his knees and grunted but kept a firm grip on the weapon as well. The flashlight fell from Wiley's fingers, breaking with a crash on the concrete. During their struggle for the hatchet, Ethan held tight to his own flashlight, the beam dancing aimlessly in every direction. An occasional flash revealed the moccasin still coiled and hissing, its tail now vibrating like a reed. With one final yank, Wiley ripped the hatchet from the hand of his younger brother, and in the recoil, the cast iron ripped across the rocky ceiling. Sparks showered in the darkness.

Wiley turned mad in the eyes toward the snake, which hissed as the boy taunted it with the hatchet. Ethan held his light with both hands, pointing it steadily at the moccasin for his brother's sake. After awkwardly readying himself in the narrow tunnel, Wiley leapt forward in a crouched position and whipped the weapon at the body of the serpent. He missed only by a fraction, and as he struck the left wall, the cottonmouth sprang forward and bit through Wiley's thin t-shirt into the back of his sunburned shoulder.

Wiley's screams echoed about the tunnel from end to end. He spun around, grabbing blindly for the whipping snake.

"Hold still!" Ethan shouted.

Wiley obeyed. Ethan shined the light on the head of the serpent. Venom and blood soaked into Wiley's white shirt. With the caution of a surgeon, Ethan clutched the snake by the neck as if to strangle it before jerking it loose. The sharp fangs tore deep gashes down Wiley's back. Ethan pinned the viper with his left hand and cut off its head with the hatchet.

Wiley staggered towards the entrance, but his adrenaline carried him less than halfway before he collapsed onto his hands and knees. Lee was inaudibly yelling from outside the tunnel. Dropping the hatchet, Ethan held the flashlight with his teeth and began to pull and drag his larger brother. Ethan's head scraped the ceiling, and his elbows banged against the concrete walls with every tug. Wiley moaned in pain.

Lee met them near the entrance, but at his height and in his position, there was little he could do but man the flashlight and lead the way out. Ethan fell once, then twice, scraping most of the skin off of his knees.

Finally, the trio popped from the tunnel like corks. Dogs were still barking and the sun was falling away quickly. Ethan removed his shirt and pressed it on Wiley's wound. "What should we do, Lee? Should we suck out the venom or what?"

Lee thought. "No, don't suck it out. It's too late for that, ain't no use. All we can do is keep the wound below the heartbeat. We gotta carry him back tilted head down."

Ethan dropped the bloody shirt. Lee grasped Wiley under the arms and lifted him as Ethan raised up Wiley's legs as high as he could. To ease the strain, he attempted to prop Wiley's ankles on his shoulders, but Ethan's left foot slipped on a patch of algae. The weight of the fall was absorbed entirely by his tailbone, rendering him stiff for a moment while he sat, helpless, in the wet grass.

"Switch places with me," Lee said. "I'm taller and can hold his legs higher! Get up, quick! Let's switch!"

After the change, Ethan allowed his hands to do most of the work, gripping the armpits of his brother as best he could without pressing directly on the wound. The sun burned his bare chest as a mockingbird swooped low, warning them to keep away from its nest. Through it all, Wiley forced his head up to look forward. At last, they reached the rebar ladder.

"What do we do, Lee?"

"I can climb it," insisted Wiley.

Ethan and Lee nodded to each other. They let Wiley try, but he lost his grip about halfway to the top. One foot slipped and then a hand. Ethan pinned him to the ladder as Lee raced to the top and yanked him up. Wiley lay limp like a corpse on the grassy edge, and as the boys dragged him under the twisted metal fence, the rusty spikes scraped across Ethan's bare back. With what strength they had left, they carried the whimpering Wiley into the house through the back door.

Ethan's mother lounged on the couch in the family room, while his father was in the same position Ethan had left him, passed out and snoring in the living room on the opposite side of the wall between the two bodies. When the boys stumbled in, she jumped up, shouting, "Dear God, dear Lord! What happened?" They dropped Wiley on the floor. Misunderstanding at first, she first put her arms around Ethan. Lee went to the kitchen and grabbed the landline off the wall to call for help.

"Not me, Mama, not me," Ethan cried out. "Wiley, he's been bit on his shoulder, Mama, by a moccasin. I'm so sorry, Mama!"

Wiley rolled on his side, moaning. His ripped flesh was exposed, and blood seeped down to the bottom of his t-shirt.

"I can't see nothing, Mama," said Wiley. "It's all blurry, Mama."

Turning him on his back, she knelt down beside him. "You'll be okay, honey, you'll be okay," she said with the instinct of a mother and the experience of a nurse.

Lee finished the call, ran in, and raised Wiley's legs up, pointing them towards the crucifix on the mantle as a sofa cushion was propped under his back. Ethan's mother wiped Wiley's brow with her hand. Wiley began to convulse as their father stirred awake.

"What in the hell happened?" he cried out, blinking his eyes. He stared at Wiley, whose body was once more still. "What did you do, Ethan?"

"He's been bit by a snake!" retorted the mother. "I leave them in your care, and look what happens!"

"I never meant—" their father began.

"You drunk, " their mother shouted. "Don't you care about your boys?"

As the pair argued, Wiley let out a sputtering breath and looked up into Ethan's face.

"Ethan," he whispered. "Ethan."

The younger brother bent down and lowered his bloody ear close to the beckoning blue lips.

"Daddy ain't never told me I'm a man," Wiley admitted. "I made that up to get at you, and now

I'm gonna die for it!" His eyes filled with tears and ran down his face, mixing with the beads of sweat. "I'm sorry."

Ethan clutched his brother's cheeks. "You ain't gonna die," said Ethan. "And I forgive you if you forgive me, but I swear you ain't gonna die!" Wiley nodded and reached out to grip his brother's hand.

Their father loomed over them like a black cloud, his voice rising. "Ethan, you suck out that poison, and you suck it out now!"

That ain't gonna work," replied Lee, who was holding Wiley's legs steady. "It's way too late for that now. You ain't gonna get that venom out."

Excuse me, child, excuse me!"

I'm just telling you, ain't gonna work."

"Get out! Out! Get outta my house! You think I don't know what's best for my own son? Out!"

With that, Lee pulled the glass-top coffee table around to the side of the couch and rested Wiley's legs along the length of it. As the boy exited the front door, a distant siren wailed.

"Daddy, they're almost here," pleaded Ethan. "The rescue people, they're coming."

The father stepped over Wiley to retrieve a pair of scissors from a kitchen drawer, which he used to cut open Wiley's blood-soaked shirt.

"Son, dammit, I'm ordering you to suck out the poison. Now do it!"

Spittle dribbled from the side of Wiley's mouth, and he panted like an exhausted dog. His skinny body shuddered once more. Ethan stared at his brother, not knowing what to do.

When Ethan turned Wiley over, his feet slipped off the coffee table and thumped onto the floor. As Ethan's mouth neared the wound, his mother gripped his shoulders and pulled him away.

"No, son," she said to her youngest. Looking up into the hazel eyes of her husband, she commanded, "You do it."

The father chuckled, but his expression revealed his uncertainty.

"This is it," she said as she stood. "Bend down there and suck that venom out, if you think it'll help, or else get out and stay out."

"You can't make me do nothing 'cause—"

"Out!" barked the mother, but the father didn't move.

Stomping her foot and pointing to the door, she yelled the word once more before adding, "Don't you dare come back or call 'til you're good and sober! Out!"

Throwing his arms up, the father surrendered. As if looking for something of value to pawn, he swept the Paul Bunyan decanter off of the mantle before exiting through the back door. Seconds later, the front door flew open.

Where is the victim?" came a voice from the foyer.

In here!" yelled their mother as she stooped low once more over her children.

While the paramedic assessed the wound, two others lifted a stretcher out of the ambulance and carried it through the front door to Wiley.

"Should we suck out the venom?" asked the mother.

"Oh, no," replied the paramedic, now administering antivenin. "Within seconds after a bite, that is useless, not to mention dangerous." He checked Wiley's pupils again and measured his pulse. "Don't worry, ma'am. He's going to be sick for a while, but he should make it." Pausing a moment, he glanced at their mother. "If you tried to suck it out, you could have been poisoned too."

Wiley was placed gently onto the stretcher and then wheeled headfirst through the foyer and out the front door into a stable wind. The mother walked beside her son, pulling Ethan along by the hand and dabbing her tears with her uniform sleeve. The three squeezed into the back of the ambulance before the doors slammed shut.

At last, Ethan was left to examine his injuries: a ring of cuts and bruises around his skull, slashes down his back, and skin scraped off of his hands and knees. His muscles, weary from the ordeal, stiffened. He laid his head on his mother's bony shoulder as the siren screamed.

They careened around the corner, and Ethan caught a glimpse of his father sitting at the bus stop. The decanter lay shattered at his feet, and his shoulders shook as he sobbed like a widower. Ethan waved subtly, and as his father raised his head, their mutual gaze stretched the length of the road. Ethan turned and whispered into his mother's ear, "He'll be back, Mama. I think he'll be back."

She stroked Ethan's brow. "Not yet, son," she said. "He has his own poisons." She hummed as Ethan fell asleep.

Ephphatha

This morning, the boy bathed for the first time since his mother failed to wake up four days ago. It was good to be alone. Micah pushed a bar of soap at a steady speed along the rim of the tub like a tank set on invading the three plastic army men stationed against the tile wall. In these last few days, he had been cornered in the center of attention by the stream of visitors. It was the act of normalcy, the pretending without any play, that absolutely exhausted his energy. When the water cooled and lost its comfort, Micah pulled the plug. He watched as her last hug, rinsed from his skin, swirled down the drain with the dirty water.

For good reason, Micah and his father arrived at the funeral home over an hour early that Friday morning, and it was wise of him to ensure that at no point was the coffin to be on wheels. It was a cold, cold place, a pixelated image of a building inside as much as out. Save for the gifted flowers framed about the body, the room was deprived of anything that could be called beautiful. His mother's coffin sprung from the gray-white walls and once-maroon carpet like an altar. In Micah's imaginings of this moment, he never once pictured what he now saw: the casket was open.

"I want to see her," he whispered to his father, who retrieved a metal chair from the corner and set it before the coffin. Micah climbed and looked down on the body of his mother. The daily advice of his father bounded from side to side amidst the web of his thoughts: *Clear your mind.* She was still, perfectly still, as if silence could be a cadaver.

"Can I lay with her?"

Micah's father shook his head.

At first, it was all science. He thought of the brown toads that died in his glass jars or the skins of locusts that clung to pine trees, but unlike their disposable forms, there was something like life left in her. Might she smile any moment at the sound of his voice or shed a tear? He reached for her wrist, soft. He closed his eyes and fingered the macaroni necklace bundled up in her palm.

"Mama," he whimpered, "I know you can hear me! Can you hear me, mama?" He gripped her wrist, which was as soft as ever. "I miss you, mama!" It all happened so quickly. *Clear your mind, son!*

At the sight of his floating tie, Micah's father leaned away from his son and against the coffin, and if not for his weight, it may have tumbled on top of them both. The mountains of flowers about the room rattled as if by a stiff breeze before falling prostrate before the boy. Petals snapped from their buds and lodged against his small frame. *Not again!* Micah released his mother's arm, which floated as if reaching for him and jumped backward. As he crawled away from the coffin, the metal chair collapsed and crept across the old carpet as if preying upon him. Petals swatted from his face and struck him in the chest and back.

"It's all my fault!" He hadn't meant to say it out loud. "I'm a freak; I did this to her!" At this lie, the petals dropped from his body, and the chair died in the center of the room. He stood up and pinned himself against the cold wall: *Breathe.* His father steadied the coffin, returned the wrist to where it first lay and strode across the petals. Micah was peeled from the wall; his sweat was left glistening on the gray paint.

As Micah's father disentangled the macaroni necklace from his hair, Micah noticed the new neighbor girl who stared about the room through frazzled black hair. She was clinging to the doorframe in the corner. The boy broke their eye contact so that his tears might go unnoticed as he was led from the room to freshen up.

✠

Micah's father had stopped caring how late Micah was out with friends in the neighborhood, just like he stopped caring about nearly everything. Now, straddling the branch of a satsuma tree in his neighbor's side yard, Micah wondered if he even had any friends left. Though wanted because of his athleticism, his career in Capture the Flag and other games would have to be over. He knew that Hunter cheated by planting the flag in his shirt before placing it in plain sight only upon winning the game. They were on the same team.

"Shut up, snitch!" Hunter yelled at Micah when the truth was revealed.

"You just don't want to lose to a girl," Micah retorted. Meredith was on the other team. When two or three of them threatened him, Micah stood his ground. The game's flag flew from Hunter's hand and stuck to Micah's hip. That's when Micah ran, but not so fast that the shrills of the boys calling him a freak could not catch up.

"What are you doing up in that tree?" Meredith asked. "I've been looking for you everywhere."

Micah said nothing.

"Thank you for defending me."

Again, it was quiet but not still. The hair on Meredith's head rose up as if from slumber and stretched in the boy's direction. Branches from the tree bent in upon themselves and a few leaves snapped away.

"I don't think you're a freak."

"You should, because I am! You've seen it for yourself twice." Slowly the branches and hair subsided. Micah climbed out of the tree but not without his share of cuts.

"I'll walk you home," Meredith said, and the two slumped away in the direction of Micah's house a block over.

✠

He knew it wasn't her first time drinking; that much was obvious. When Micah learned she had chosen the same college as him the hair on his neck shot out and his spine tingled. She fit in with the dozens of animals crawling room to room, many unknowingly, like a drunken instinct on display. It was a jungle under a roof. Two hours in and Micah and Meredith were dancing to country music next to the pool table.

They stopped with the music.

"Really gooood," came out of Micah's mouth like the grunt of a boar. Her smile was perfectly innocent, he thought, perfect because she was innocent. He reached for her hair, and, for a few seconds, examined it: delicate, thin, lovely. He spoke again. "Really *great* to see you."

"You, too," she slurred through a smile.

Micah put his arms around her thin waist, to which her eyes gave permission, and he lifted her onto the pool table. Her legs hung over the edge as if lifeless, and while moving between them, he kissed her thin lips. Meredith tasted like beer, and he was embarrassed that he must have tasted the same, if not worse.

She followed him to his room. He sat on the bed and she in his lap. Meredith leaned into his ear as he kissed her neck.

"I know it's been a long time, but I remember," she whispered.

Though their lips were apart for the moment, he couldn't keep his hands from her tight frame.

"Remember what?"

"Your secret."

She volleyed kisses back onto his neck as it came back to him, all of it. The rush of memories, the smell of a corpse, the empty home. It had been so long since a relapse that he had almost forgotten it was in him, the freak part. Maybe it was dead, killed by years, but he remembered her then beneath the thorny tree, hair rising almost magnetically as twigs snapped.

Within moments, she was on the other side of the threshold alone, his bedroom door in her face and locked. The smell of her lingered in the air, and he hid from it under the covers. Was he a coward? Was it still in him after all these years? These thoughts swirled about his mind like a squall. How could he not want to see her, to be with her, she who was right, who did know his secret? Would she take him back as he was? To these thoughts, Micah fell asleep.

When the movie ended, they turned off the television and sat up from their pallet of blankets on the floor. They lay back on the floor of her living room, face to face, each held up by an elbow.

"Tell me about your mom."

"Well, she died when I was ten."

"Is that it?"

"Just about."

"How'd your father handle it?"

Micah's arm was falling asleep. "Fine, I guess." He plopped onto his back and looked up at her.

"What's your relationship with him like?" she said as her hair tickled his face.

"What's your deal with all these probing questions?" He tucked her hair behind her ear.

"I just want to know more about you."

"About all my problems, you mean."

"Yes."

"Why?"

"Is there some other way in?"

He knew there was, but he didn't want to go there. Even in the dark, their eyes met. Micah felt her grip his hand as she lay flat next to him. Her skin was soft and warm like bread. "We'll have to trade," he said.

"Trade what?"

"Problems."

"Fine, you first. You know I'd share anything with you, even a coffin, if it came down to it. Tell me first, though, what happened with your mother?"

Micah bit his lip to kill the tears. "Heart attack," was all he could mutter. It was her turn.

"I'm adopted. My birth mother didn't want me, and still, as far as I know, doesn't want anything to do with me. All I know is I wasn't supposed to happen, but here I am!"

For a while, silence. A car approached outside and passed but not before briefly illuminating her face with its headlights. Oh, how beautiful, how real and humble she was. If he couldn't tell her the truth, then truth might as well not exist.

"My father and I talk often enough only because we have to," Micah said. "You know, just to coordinate money or trips home. We've talked to each other a lot but haven't really spoken in years. He doesn't know that I know about his drug problem."

"I love you," she said.

Before Micah could say it back, he thought it over first. Even in the dark, he knew what was happening. The cup of water on the coffee table fell over, and within fragments of a second, his shirt was wet. He had to say it.

"I love you too."

Once it was off his lips, he knew that he needed something, something inside him, to cancel it out. *Clear your mind; make way for other thoughts.* He felt it and let the lust burst forth and carry him away, and in doing so, slipped his hand under the back of her shirt.

✠

Would she be a freak, too? This was Micah's incessant worry, a haunting anxiety that plagued the entirety of his time. The traditional worries of becoming a father, like the deprivation of sleep and freedom, were like ripples on the wave of this horrific possibility.

Meredith was showing, and her attitude balanced the scale of the tone of the home. She would often sit with her hand over her stomach, gently humming, rocking back and forth like love incarnate. She knew his thoughts but never invaded them. He, in the meantime, bounced from room to room, fidgeting with his wedding ring and cleaning and rearranging anything but himself.

"Oh!" Meredith gasped. "Quick, Micah, come here!"

Micah rushed to the room. His worries were disarmed by her smile.

"I could feel her kick! Put your hand right here!"

Meredith grabbed Micah's hand and settled it warmly on her womb. A few moments of silence passed, then *bump bump*, at which point, Micah gazed into Meredith's eyes. How beautiful they were! Would this baby have her mother's eyes, full of a hope and kindness so needed in the world? He couldn't pull his hand away from his baby. Did he just think that? *His baby*! Would it matter if she got the freak part but shared in even an ounce of the goodness of her mother?

Bump. The beautiful face before him melted, sucked away from her rising hair. In his newfound love of the child, for a few moments, he did not understand what was happening. Meredith's lower jaw fell open, and her breath ceased. Meredith sliced away his hand, stood up and wrapped both palms around her baby. It was not long before the bleeding started. By the time they arrived at the hospital, it was too late; the sonogram confirmed the worst.

✠

"Well, now or never!" she exclaimed as soon as he scraped his corpse across the threshold. The rustle of the divorce papers pushed across the dining room table was like a knife slicing through the air, set on murder. Her free hand, as it had been for these last few months, cradled what had once been the resting place of their child. Oh, how fitting it should end like this! A cold moment for a cold house. Like the phantom he was, Micah glided to the pen and scribbled his name like a toddler across the paper. Micah couldn't bear the thought of being in the same building, let alone the same room, when it came for her turn. He guessed he was supposed to see that she had yet to sign, and he guessed he was supposed to read into it somehow.

"I guess this is goodbye."

One foot he put in front of the other, a dishonorable discharge. The front door creaked with grief on his way out. On the whole, a lovely evening, save for the screaming sky. The flames of the sun spewed to the heavens like so many flying arrows, red from war. A few thin clouds retreated eastward behind the silhouette of small birds strung on a power line. With a loose hand, Micah gripped the top of the mailbox and swung onto the sidewalk in the direction of the bloody sun.

Micah knew this was best, and he knew that Meredith knew. She would sign the papers as leisurely as he now strode away from her once and for all. No, he knew her better than that. *Let's be honest,* he thought. *Honest.* She was dead inside, dead, sipping that poisonous alcohol day after day since it happened. She was a tomb now, gray and empty since he killed their child. He had no words to spare for her, let alone life to give.

He kicked a pebble; *tap tap tap tap tap.* Life, new life. For these last few months, they were two dead people trying to breathe life into one another, swindlers swapping snake oil.

His mother had the easy way out. Why couldn't he? When they finally put her in the dirt, his father turned to painkillers, then later his wife to alcohol, and finally, he, as always, to the recesses of his solitude.

What he wanted was death. No, death was not the right word. What is death when you're already dead? His mother had not died but transitioned. His father then was dead, as was Meredith. This was his destiny; this, too, was his path. Even now, he was killing himself, the crescendo of his lifelong suicide attempt. He saw his funeral, not well attended, unlike his mother's.

Tap tap tap tap tap tap. He stopped shy of the pebble. There had been something, just now, to

35

lift him into the dining room. At the center of the table, he now saw it again right behind the papers: the empty whiskey bottle, and in it, the blooming branch of a Satsuma. The centerpiece was a physical cadence, an obvious riddle, an archetype of where they had been and come from. The copper vapors and subtle, white blooms demanded an answer: would he want to see this to its logical end?

He turned around with his back to the sun, which had since soaked the entirety of the sky in its blood. She had given him the freedom to make a choice. She had had all day to sign and had not. Choice! The destiny he had pictured for himself, the destiny he had pictured for his wife, were his choice. His chest and ears and lungs were opened, like an unexpected breath when drowning seems inevitable. He stepped in the direction of home.

"Meredith! Meredith! Open the door!" he cried out. *Tap tap tap* came the pebble at his heels. *Clear your mind; stay calm. Listen!* The advice of his father entered into him like breath, a lifetime's habit. *Listen!* Listen. Every breath was short. He could indeed see his future, his funeral, the one coffin. He lifted a hand to wipe the sweat from his brow, but as he shook it off, the droplets arched back onto his frame. Grass bent his way. The new leaves of spring, small but stout, began to snap from their branches.

Meredith must have felt it. He saw her emerge onto the porch. Her hair enveloped her worn yet lovely face. She gripped the peeling banister and bent her knees to brace herself. He had never seen her so vulnerable.

As Micah passed the mailbox, it snapped and struck him in the back, causing him to fall. Micah was quickly to his feet and again running, if it could be called running. Trotting, or perhaps upright crawling, he made his way to the porch. Whole trees about the front yard threatened to snap. Insects, butterflies, sticks, toys from the neighbor's front yard, and other things scattered about raced in his direction, flying or rolling over the flat grass. The car in the driveway shook. With an otherworldly effort, Micah ascended the stairs of the porch and shoved the creaking front door open and shut as if in a hellish squall.

Meredith clung to the doorway on the other side of the foyer. Cushions started to break loose with blankets and trinkets. Cabinet doors were thrown open in the kitchen.

"I love you," Micah said. "You were always there, always there for me! Remind me what I need to hear to make this stop because I can't do this alone!"

Meredith relaxed her grip on the wall and was thrust into his arms just before the cushions pummeled the pair. Plates and glasses from the kitchen crashed into walls, and pieces of ceramic and shattered glass crept out of the kitchen and gripped the ball of home that kissed on the floor. She ripped her lips from his.

"I love you too," she said. The very words came to him, into him, were now a part of him. Their embrace resumed. When the walls began to shake, their eyes met and knew there was no other way, no going back. The sofa, the dining room table, all of it was piled on. Even on the night of the party, they hadn't kissed like this, a kiss with meaning. Now there was no kissing, only unity, and by the time the first wall fell, they were sharing even more than blood or bones.

Memento Mori

The One Thing Necessary

Alexander sank into the Adirondack chair and folded his cold hands into the warmth of his torso. His thoughts drifted as they often did at times like this to his friends, who were probably studying for midterms. He had flunked out of college and had nothing better to do than to roast marshmallows with his sister Alana on her 17th birthday. Alexander could tolerate nearly every annoyance, from the cold that stung his dry hands to the black bangs that scratched his green eyes, except for her. It could have been that she was the white sheep of the family or something more simple. Alexander may have been quiet and teetering on the edge of his parents' expectations, but he had dreams too. He had ideas. If Alana had dreams, they were probably superficial, like daydreams. He purposefully sat opposite her with the fire between them. The intimacy of a statement as trite as "Happy birthday, Alana" was too personal. Their only other sibling, seven-year-old Tripp, was much more tolerable to live with.

Across the yard, their home was well-lit on the inside, and his parents were busying themselves in and around the kitchen. Tripp was standing on a chair at the table, dipping a brush into every color of paint as if he could sketch a rainbow with one stroke. His parents lifted their heads like deer at what must have been the doorbell. While his father inched towards the door, his mother scrambled about the kitchen for those last few seconds, practically throwing knives and bowls off of the counter and into the sink. Cynthia and Louise had arrived. His father greeted the two girls and gave them side hugs before showing them to the back door. Once outside, Louise's feet became tangled in Cynthia's, and they both stumbled and nearly fell. Alana jumped from her chair and ran to meet her two best friends. Alexander thought to himself that this could be the furthest she had run in her entire life.

"Happy birthday! Happy, happy, happy birthday!" Cynthia and Louise exclaimed as they wrapped their arms around his sister. Both of them were six inches taller than Alana but at least ten pounds lighter. Just then, the speakers hanging outside of the home came to life, which awoke Alexander from malicious thoughts about his sister, thoughts so deep that his marshmallow was fully caught up in the flames and as black as the darkness that crept in upon them. A country twang reverberated through the night across the yard, giving rhythm to the flames as they danced. The girls stilled and stared at one another. "Nick Roh!" Alana said. All three sang along:

Alexander rolled his eyes and shoved his hands even more deeply into the pockets of his navy blue jacket after throwing his roasting stick into the flames. *One person singing this song was enough*, he thought. From one of the pockets, he pulled a folded piece of computer paper. He straightened it out and stared into one of his sketches, framed into four segments like a comic book. The man in the image bent his head low as his arms grew longer and longer, eventually wrapping the earth. Alexander crumpled the art and threw it into the fire as well, and he watched with a hint of regret as the paper melted into the glowing coals. Alana saw but seemed to think nothing of it. After a few minutes, the music quieted, and the girls chirped like nightingales about the country star. Not only was he handsome but eligible. He had recently played shows all across New England and was making his way south along the East Coast. Alexander's angst boiled in him until he yelled out, "Nick

Ruuuuuhhhhh. What kind of a name is that? How do you even pronounce it?"

After only a moment's pause, the girls ignored him as if he were a grasshopper chiming from the trees behind them.

"I'll bet it's not even his real name. I'll bet it's a made-up celebrity name. They've all got 'em, you know!" Alexander decided this was worth exposing his hands to the cold yet again. He pulled out his smartphone to look him up. Very quickly, he came upon the truth, which was sure to crush his sister and ruin her birthday.

"It's not even his real name. I have the proof right here!" he said through the flames, which began to die down. He was practically salivating at this opportunity. "His real name is Nicholas Rigotta. He's Italian, for crying out loud! You can't get much less country than that!"

"His father was born in Italy," Alana said, a bit like a snake, with a lisp like a hiss that whistled through her braces and round cheeks. On special occasions like this, she ditched her glasses for contact lenses, which bothered her eyes more than they did for most people. The firelight glowed in the tears brought on by the irritation. "He, on the other hand, was born in Alabama!" There was definitude in this. It was almost as if she had researched the man simply to make Alexander look a fool.

"Glad to see you're well-educated in the things that really matter," Alexander retorted.

"Go back to college, Alexander! Oh wait, you can't; you flunked out!" Alana said. "And make yourself useful and put more logs on the fire for my birthday."

Alexander clenched his teeth and retreated deeply into himself in search of a remark that would crush her. It couldn't be found. If Alana's snickering friends weren't around, he would flick a coal or two at her and call it an accident.

Mockingly, he scraped a handful of pine straw off of the cold ground and tossed it onto the fire. The bundle flashed a crisp yellow light across the fresh-cut grass, but it was swallowed by the golden waves crashing all around in only a few moments.

Tripp, who had watched him out of the kitchen window, sprinted out the back door with a flashlight and began to gather straw from around the yard. Over and over, he threw it into the flames and each time took a step back as if he had tossed in a can of gasoline. After a while, he became bored and started poking at the fire with a long stick.

As the tension between Alexander and Alana subsided, their parents came through the back door carrying a cake. Seventeen candles shined together like a torch in the night and illuminated their father's smiling face. After all of the singing, the cake was cut by the mother and distributed as the father carefully placed three new logs into the fire pit. Alexander watched to see if his sister would eat more than one piece. He was disappointed when she didn't.

"Were you able to get the concert tickets, dear?" their father asked Alana after dabbing his mouth with a napkin.

"No," she said as she peered at the ground and crossed her legs at the ankles. "I already told you that they sold out in less than five minutes, and online, they're now triple the price, even for the worst seats."

"Well, what are you going to do next Wednesday night instead?"

"I don't know, just homework, I guess."

"Whatever you do, do not make plans!" their father said through a smile. From his pants pocket, he pulled an envelope. It read, "FOR MY ALANA."

"Shut up, shut up, shut up!" Alana said. She ripped the envelope from his hands and tore it open. She pulled out four tickets:

NICK ROH IN CONCERT
LIVE FROM THE JEFFERSON COUNTY CIVIC CENTER
BIRMINGHAM, AL

As if it were planned, the three girls screamed in unison and danced around the fire. They drifted around the flames and, like a whirlwind, sucked up to their father to thank him. Her joy was like acid rain to Alexander. He had to get out of here; he had to make it back to college. Even the community college in town had small apartments he could rent, but school was never his talent. If he weren't embarrassed by his artwork, he could do more of it and maybe sell a piece or two. That might make his mom proud in her own maternal fashion, but his father would just as quickly turn his back on the idea.

"Daddy, why are there four tickets?" Alana asked.

Alexander chuckled to himself before asking Alana why she didn't have enough friends to take to the concert of the year. Everyone ignored him.

"Well, honey, it was my plan to go with you," said the father. "Birmingham is quite a drive, especially with all that traffic downtown. Not to mention, it's a school night."

"Okay, daddy," Alana said, a bit dissatisfied that a parent would be accompanying them to a concert.

"However," the father said as if it were a disappointment, "I have a board meeting that night and won't be able to make it after all." Alexander saw to his fright that his father cast him a sideways glance.

"No, please, please, no," Alexander whispered to himself. The hair on his arms stood straight up, and his mouth hung open like a window.

"Your mother, as you know, has bridge group on the first Wednesday of each month, and it's her month to host," said the father. "So, that means that she can't go either."

Alana had a sense of what was coming as well

and began to propose solutions. "I promise I'll drive carefully, and none of us will fall asleep in the car. Never once, not even one time, has the GPS on my phone been wrong. It's always gotten me to where I need to go." Her father put up his hand and opened his mouth, but she continued. "Last year on my sixteenth birthday, Mom gave me a can of mace that I can slip into my purse in case anyone tries to mess with us, and all of us will make sure our phones are charged all the way."

Cynthia and Louise nodded and opened their eyes wide as if to prove that they could stay awake all night.

Like an honest judge, the father considered all the evidence, but in the end, he fell back on what was surely his proposal from the beginning. "No, honey, no, I'm not sending you to Birmingham by yourself. Your brother will go with you, and—"

Alexander stood to protest, but his father cut him off.

"—and if he doesn't, then he can move out of my home and, since he can't seem to find work, start searching under rocks to find money for college next year."

There was nothing Alexander could say. It was finalized. He and Alana looked at one another and crept back to their chairs. Tripp was running as fast as he could around the fire until his mother swooped him away for a bath. After a few minutes of silence, Alexander stood up and shouted a sarcastic good night before slinking off to his room. He made sure to drag his feet across the pavers and slam the back door.

✠

Close to sleep and in the near dark of night, Alexander had finally fallen into his comfort. Sitting at his small desk, paper spread before him, the light of the lamp casting an oval across the wood, mechanical pencil in hand; this was the purpose of his time. Over and again, he clicked the lead and pressed the tip into the desktop. This habit had a way of soothing and clearing the mind like a plumber clears a pipe. His life was like that, a clog. Over and again, he had fallen, fallen into a pit, finding himself in the muddy bottom, stuck and unsure of the next move. Through every ditch that Alexander had scraped through in life, from academics to pleasing parents and staying out of trouble, there stretched a bridge for his sister. He had failed in college, nearly every class. Now, his sister was closer to living the college life than he, closer to the success offered by the world.

The next morning, Alexander was called and offered part-time work at the local hardware store, a position he accepted to keep his father off of his back. Although it paid only minimum wage, he enjoyed his labors most of the time. Typically he was set to work on some project, from spray-painting outdoor furniture to sweeping and mopping, which gave him plenty of time to think.

At first, it was with dread that he passed the hours closer and closer to the date of the concert. He invented mental games to make the time pass more slowly, as if he could push the drive to Birmingham further and further into the future. He paced his steps to the rhythm of two seconds each and counted the tiles on the floor and the bricks on the wall. After a few days, however, he began to look forward to the opportunity of being a killjoy to the evening simply by his presence. Not only that, but he could also make his sister drive. She was a terrible driver and had already, more than once, sideswiped a passing car driving on a major highway.

Eventually, the day of the concert arrived. Alexander had been home since noon and was shocked away from his art when the three teenage girls burst through the back door and slammed it shut. Their squealing pierced the walls like radiation and rung in his ears. He had been working on this piece for days. The man with the long arms looked into the heavens as if to ask, "Why me?" His arms rolled over hills and through villages. Major cities had to build bridges over them, and a few hearts were pierced by one of his hands. Pigeons built their nests nearby and perched along them as if he might scatter a bag of breadcrumbs. Children balanced on the arms like tightropes, and bureaucrats nailed citations and warrants and warnings to them so the people would know how unwelcome they were in that place. One police officer tried to saw it off but could not cut through the bone. After a few more minutes, the cartoon was complete. Alexander bent low and blew along the paper. Excess bits of lead and rubber were damned to the crack between the desk and the wall.

With a smirk, the artist signed his name in the bottom corner, and as he stood up to admire the finished product, he heard his name being yelled by his mother. She needed to talk to him, she said. Maybe she'd like to see it? Maybe this was the time to show her? Yes, he would have to start with her; he would make the work appear to be something more casual than reality, like a hobby. Yes, mother, he would say, I have been working on these things in my spare time; yes, father, would say, it is a waste of time; no, I don't care. He slipped his work into a manila envelope and tucked it like contraband into the inside sleeve of his navy coat.

At the bottom of the stairs, he had only to follow the sounds of bustle and stress like breadcrumbs to the kitchen to find his mother. The room looked like a small pottery outlet. Vases were lined up along the counter; platters of all colors had been pulled from cabinets unopened for months and now were spread across the island.

She was splattering crackers and cheese with strawberry jam and, having sensed his presence, began to speak without turning around to face him. "Tonight, please be careful, dear."

"I'll think about it."

As if he needed to know, she began to relay the details of the evening. Tripp was spending the night out at their cousin's house, and the ladies would begin to arrive around 6:15. Where they would put their purses and coats, she did not yet know. Maybe they could spread them out on the bed, unless it was raining. In that case, she would need every hook on the coat rack. Without warning, scarves and jackets and hats and sweaters, only one of which belonged to Alexander, were piling up in his arms. His mother ordered him upstairs with them all and to put them in the proper place. She needed to run to the store and the florist before coming back and making final preparations. If the women were still there when they returned from Birmingham, they were to come into the living room and say hello no matter how tired they were. Unless they smelled like smoke. In that case, they should not come in.

"One last thing," she said. "You're driving tonight, your father's orders. Tonight is for Alana and her friends; do not ruin it." She then scooped up her purse and two trays to put in the garage refrigerator on the way out.

Alexander climbed the stairs and dumped the pile at Alana's bedroom door, knocked twice, and went back down to steal an *hors d'oeuvre*. He sank into the leather sofa to rest, placing the burden of leaving on time entirely upon the shoulders of his sister.

✠

He did not know how long he slept. His eyes cracked open to see Alana shaking the car keys and yelling to get up. When he finally did, he stretched, and Alana caught a glance of the manila envelope.

"What's that?" she asked.

"What's what?"

"In your coat, what is that?"

"Crack cocaine, what do you care?"

"Ha, hurry up, it's time to go!"

He dared not leave the envelope in the house for fear that one of his family members, now knowing it existed, would search his room until it was found. Alexander stepped into the vehicle with a careful hand over his coat so as not to bend the art that was pinned to his rib cage. Alana grunted as he began to back out of the driveway before Cynthia and Louise had a chance to open the door. "Just a joke," he said, and they drove off.

It was a beautiful evening. Alexander rolled the windows down despite the protests of the three girls who had already done their hair. The cool air was refreshing. He breathed in and filled his lungs as if he could capture the peace of the moment and let it out when he would need it most at the concert. Before long, they were on the interstate, where the brisk air rushed through the car and threatened to send loose receipts and other papers flying out into the world. Alexander rolled up the windows.

"I have something for you, Alana!" said Cynthia. She opened a plastic bag sitting at her feet and drew out four t-shirts, one for each of them. "I didn't think you'd wear one, Alexander, but I didn't want you to feel left out."

"I need something to blow my nose into anyway," he said with a laugh that was not echoed by any of the girls.

Alana rushed to pull the shirt down over her head, but for a few moments, it was stuck to her face. She looked like a cartoon character or a pagan deity with the body of a person and the head of an animal. Alexander held back his laughter. It was a dark gray t-shirt, which on the back displayed the dates of all of Nick Roh's tour stops for the year. On the front was the cover art for his new album, which was a large red fig leaf twisted slightly into the shape of a heart. When she finally pulled it down around her neck, she gripped the symbol and pressed it to her own heart as if hers and Nick's were one.

"What if he sees me?" Louise said from the backseat.

"No, no, what if he sees *me*?" Alana asked.

"If he makes eye contact with me, I might just fall over and die!" Cynthia said.

Alexander let his head crash against the driver's side window like he would welcome falling asleep at the wheel. The yellow needle of the speedometer hovered just above the speed limit and bounced a bit with the hills. Alexander pressed the gas and pushed his luck. He had to get there. At least at the concert, he could excuse himself to the bathroom and wait outside for most of the show. An old woman rocking on a front porch raised her arm at the automobile, but if she was waving to him or cursing his speed, Alexander could not tell. He waved back, envious of the freedom that the evening had bestowed upon her.

"I bet I can get a kiss," Alana said. "If he knew me really for who I am and let me love him, then I know he'd love me back and give me a kiss." At this, the girls in the back giggled until Alexander interjected.

"You've never been kissed your whole life, little sister! Tell me why you think this grown man who can get any girl he wants is gonna go out of his way to kiss you?"

"Shut up, Alexander!" Alana hissed through her braces.

"The only man that ever kissed you was Dad," Alexander said.

"Mom says you used to kiss me all the time, big brother, and I know that's the only kiss you ever got!"

"No wonder I have so much acne. I'm still waiting for the warts to pop out of my lips."

Alana opened her mouth to reply but let it go. Alexander knew what she was thinking. Be the bigger person! Mom and Dad would be so proud of her. Alana bent down and drew from her purse a CD. It was Nick Roh's newest album. "Guess what Dad gave me before we left? He said if you don't let us listen to this, then you're not going back to college." For half a minute, she struggled to open the package. The plastic was so tightly wrapped around the case that it was not easily cut or penetrated. Alana began to bite at the case like an animal until she shrieked and dropped it to the floor. With her hands cupped around her mouth, she began to cry little sobs of pain like a small child.

Cynthia and Louise each placed a hand on her shoulder and leaned through the middle of the car to ask what had happened. She put up a finger to tell them to wait and dabbed the inside of her cheek with a napkin from the glove compartment. After a few more moments, she opened her mouth and turned towards her friends. A wire as sharp as a sewing needle had broken away from her braces. The sliver of metal was protruding from her teeth and into her gums near the corner of her lips. Cynthia and Louise rattled off suggestions as to how to fix it, but Alana would hear none of it. She wouldn't touch it. It was too gross; it was too dangerous. What if she messed it up? What if she ruined her braces, costing her mother and father even more money? No, no, this was her birthday, she said, and she would enjoy the evening no matter what. If she could survive the trip with her brother, then she could survive anything. She gave Alexander a wicked glance and climbed into the back seat between her two friends. One of them wrestled the CD package open and slipped in the disc.

The first couple of songs were calming, and as Alexander receded into the comfort of his thoughts, the strain that divided the front from the back seats began to melt away. This did not last long, for the third song on the album was the same as that of the birthday party, *One Thing Necessary*. From Alexander's point of view, listening to this was only slightly preferable to crashing the car into a tree.

Playing poker with my buddies,
college football on TV,
I'd kick 'em out and shut it off if it
drove you far from me.
Snapper reeling, deep-sea fishing,
camping under country skies,
I'd cut the line and hike to town
to rid my life of alibis.

'Cause there ain't nothing, no nothing,
that can split up love or fate.
My mamma she don't understand
that life is more of give than take.
My buddies say I'm whipped;
my daddy says I best be wary.
What none of them can understand
is you're the one thing necessary!

By the time the album was half-finished, Alexander knew everything he needed to about Nick Roh. He drank more beer than water and preferred bikinis to mini-skirts. Alexander had the feeling that if he became more like this man, it would decrease the likelihood of a girlfriend, yet somehow, this superstar could be found guilty of murder, and girls would flock to him like geese. Alexander checked the rearview. The teenage girls began to awake from the ecstasy of the music as they pulled into the parking lot of the civic center.

✠

Their seats were excellent. Row 11, seats 14 through 17. They were very near the front and Louise's seat, number 17, was nearly the center of the row. Getting out of the concert through the masses of people was not going to be as easy as Alexander had anticipated. On his phone, he looked up the lineup for the evening. Any minute, the opening act, a female country artist, would play a set before introducing the legendary Nick Roh.

Amidst this crowd of music lovers, Alexander's only comforts were that there were many more girls than boys, and that if he stared at his phone from start to finish, hardly a soul would notice or care.

The emcee emerged from stage left to a raucous

applause and cheering reminiscent of a football stadium. The man tipped his cowboy hat and yelled, "How y'all doing tonight?" to even more applause. After a few more welcoming remarks and public safety regulations, he had a special announcement.

"We got something special out there for a lucky few! Something special indeed! Four, count 'em, four backstage passes to meet the man himself before the show begins." After the gasps died down, he continued, "Everyone check under your seat to see if you're the lucky winner! If it's you, don't hesitate and hurry up to the stage and show your passes to security! C'mon now!"

Within seconds, it was discovered that seats 15, 16, and 17 had nothing beneath them. Alana gazed at Alexander as if the search beneath the chairs were a matter of life and death. He reached down with a fake gasp expecting to feel nothing but metal. What he felt instead was an envelope taped to the underside of the seat. He looked up at Alana, who waited with more anticipation than parents at the birth of a child. She thought the surprised look on his face was a joke. Her cheeks sagged, and her entire person seemed to droop. If he were to ignore the envelope, none would be the wiser. Those eyes, though, his sister's eyes, changed him. They were deep and haunting for that moment, like the rough waters a man sees when thrown against the rail of a ship. He ripped away the envelope and held it out to Alana. Her scream gave it away for the entire theater. Within seconds, the foursome was displaying the passes to a security guard, who led them onto the stage and behind the thick red curtain.

The muffled voice of the emcee and the opening act became less audible as the four followed the security guard down a narrow hallway and into a waiting area. They seated themselves on a leather couch as instructed and surveyed the room. Posters from past concerts hung on the gray walls. In a far corner was a wicker bar with four or five golden vessels of alcohol. On its right, a mini fridge was stacked with red plastic cups. The room held a subtle odor, and on the coffee table before them, three cigarettes stood up straight in an ashtray. In his mind, Alexander was brought back to college but did not know if he should be elated about the memory or block it out forever. The girls either did not notice the smell or, much more likely, did not care.

The footsteps coming down the hall made the girls jump up. A hand at the doorknob put smiles across their faces, and they stood to attention like soldiers. The door was pushed open, and a young woman entered and poured a drink while ignoring the anxious fans seated before her. After a few seconds of silence, she turned and asked if they were here to see Nick and added that he's a real sweetheart. By the time she walked out the door, her glass was half empty.

After a few more anxious minutes, the security

guard asked them to stand once more. It was time, he said, to behold the man himself. The security guard pushed the door open, and Nick Roh entered the room.

"Good evening!" he said before shaking hands with all four of them. The girls were anxious to pose for a picture, but he told them there'd be plenty of time. Nick was not as put together or handsome as he appeared on television. He stumbled to the bar and poured a drink. Most of the liquor made it into the cup, but some fell off the bar and onto the carpet.

"How rude of me!" he said as he turned around to face them. "Who wants a drink? I mean, how old are y'all anyway?"

"Twenty-one," Alana spit out without hesitation.

"Twenty-one, huh?" Nick said. "Well, anyone want a drink?"

When none of them said either yes or no, he left it alone and returned to the group. Like a man who has come home from a long day of labor, he fell back into his leather seat and slumped. His left hand lazily gripped the rim of the plastic cup and, more than once, Alexander thought he was going to drop it onto the floor. His jeans were dark and tight, and his bright plaid shirt was untucked, a look that matched the top two buttons, which were undone. His arms and chest were as golden as his hair, which was as golden as the drink he finished off before setting the cup before them on a coffee table. Cynthia eyed it, clearly intending to steal it as a relic when the meeting had adjourned.

After exchanging a few pleasantries, Nick broke the ice with a question. "Can I tell you something about yourselves, ladies?" He paused to hold in a belch. "Can I tell you something about yourselves that maybe you do not even know?"

The girls leaned forward as if this man were a font of wisdom.

"The three of you," the country star continued, "are beautiful just the way you are. You know that? You can do whatever you want; you know that? This world is full of people with untapped potential. Untapped. It's asleep in them, and they don't know how to wake it up." His right hand was now on Alana's knee, and Alexander knew the thrill that must be shooting through her like an electric current. "Be bold and be beautiful, and most importantly, be you."

"It's my birthday," Alana said out of nowhere. "Well, it *was* my birthday; my dad bought us these tickets to your concert for my birthday."

"Your twenty-first birthday, huh?" Nick said, stroking her leg with a few fingers before raising them to rub his chalky eyes. "Well, happy birthday to you!" The singer winked at her then glanced at his watch and motioned to security like it was time to wrap up the meeting. After posing for pictures with the girls, he thrust one last shot down his throat and shook his head from side to side like he could toss the smell and the burn from his body.

Alexander was the first to file out, followed in line by Cynthia and Louise. Alexander glanced over his shoulder, and in a span of time that felt like something less than a moment, Nick had his arm around his sister's shoulder and nodded to security to close the door after telling his sister he had to give her a birthday present. When he tried to get back into the room, the security guard blocked him with one hand and told him to wait. Something within Alexander, something like a hangover from a more primitive time came forth. There was no time for thinking. He hit at the security guard and kicked and pushed and did all he could to get in the room. It was futile.

Seconds later, the door was flung open from the inside. The country star was muffling curses and holding his mouth as if a bee had stung him. His sister's eyes were cold and innocent, like those of a small child who had been caught up in a fight between her parents. The rough seas that Alexander had seen in them earlier had subsided and grown shallow and polluted. Her hands were folded at the navel like she was clutching a precious jewel to keep safe from a thief.

Nick took his hands off of his mouth and stuck out his bleeding and swollen tongue. "What the hell, girl! What is in your mouth? This ain't no joke! I got a performance to give. Did you bite me?" The man pushed past them and strode down the dark passageway deeper into the backstage of the arena.

The security guard saw that the girls were no threat and grabbed Alexander's hands, twisted his arms behind his back, and pushed him to a back entrance. They were being kicked out, he said, for having made an attempt to assault Mr. Roh. Cynthia, who held tightly to the plastic cup, nearly followed Nick down the passageway into the darkness. All three girls, however, followed the guard one by one, not knowing whether to comfort Alana or congratulate her on the kiss of the century. Alexander screamed a lie about how his father was a lawyer and that this wouldn't be the last time that Nick Roh or the Jefferson County Civic Center would see them.

In less than a minute, the guard shoved the big brother out the door and slammed it closed. The four of them were on the backside of the theater and would have to walk quite a distance to the car. For a minute, no one said or did anything. The silence was shattered when cheers erupted from inside. This muted applause carried with it the weight, which fell heavy like sandbags upon the girls, that they would not be attending the concert.

Nick's voice could be heard now, creeping through the cracks in the door like insects. "Good evening, Birmingham, Alabama!" he said with an added twang to more applause. "I know you're all ready to hear about my one thing necessary, but—" he was interrupted by more screams, "but first I have to apologize. A pretty little thing bit my lip backstage, but it ain't nothin' we can't get through together tonight! This first one's called *Saturday Night to Sunday Morning.*"

The bass drum kicked into rhythm and felt like punches against their chests, warning them with finality to go away. Alexander offered to go get the car, but Alana took his arm and said they'd all walk. Tears began to stream from her eyes and run her mascara, and before they reached the car, Alexander whispered to her to use his shirt. She shook her head and instead pulled up her gray t-shirt and wiped her face, leaving the fig leaf to look as if it were bleeding black.

Alana sat in the front seat on the way home. Her friends whispered a quiet sorry in a last attempt to hide their dissatisfaction at being kicked out of the concert before it even began. Alana's hands were still clenched in her lap, and she stared out the window. Alexander saw her for what must have truly been the first time. This moment of vulnerability had laid her out before him like a corpse before a mortician. This kiss, which should have thrust her into unheard-of popularity and would have built the confidence of nearly every American girl, had had the opposite effect. She felt more alone and friendless than before, at the bottom of a pit that Alexander never quite realized existed for her at all.

The two friends in the back were completely absorbed by their phones, probably posting pictures online of the encounter with the star. Alexander stretched out his arm and grabbed Alana's hands. Like plucking flower petals, he unclenched them a finger at a time and wrapped his hand around hers. She let him. When they came to a stop at an intersection, he leaned over and, descending into her vulnerability, told her that Nick was right about one thing: she was beautiful, just the way that she was, in that moment, and nothing in the world could make it more or less so. Her head turned towards his, and she nodded in approval. While he had her attention, Alexander reached into his coat, pulled out the artwork, and gave it to his sister as a belated birthday gift. She opened it, stared it over for a few minutes, slipped it back into the envelope, and slid it with care into her purse. Alexander ejected the CD and threw it out the window. It shattered on the shoulder of the highway into dozens of pieces.

Alexander dropped off the two girls at their respective houses. Cynthia unsuccessfully offered the singer's relic to Alana. Each of them, in turn, muttered some final goodbyes and sentences about how he was a jerk and that, in some ways, it was great that Alana had gotten that kiss but that they wouldn't tell anyone unless she said it was all right. Alana pretended to agree and said she'd see them at school tomorrow. It was too early to go home. If they were to show up now, they would be marched into the living room to give a report on the concert to the group of women grazing on their mother's *hors d'oeuvres.* Without asking, Alexander jerked the steering wheel to the right and parked the vehicle beneath a row of movie posters. His treat, he said.

Manhunt

If she could find him, then so could you.

You ought to have removed, at a minimum, your leather wingtip shoes and black dress socks. If you had been in your right mind, this excursion would have remained merely a curiosity or perhaps a sweet, but unrealized, possibility. Instead, it was on a Saturday in mid-March that you found yourself hugging a rockface like a fugitive along the edge of the Pigeon River. Looking skyward, you had the feeling that a single sneeze could put into motion an avalanche capable of crushing yourself to fish bait. The napkin map gripped in your left hand that Aunt Grace had hurriedly sketched on New Year's Eve at the coffee maker read the same as it did the first and fiftieth times that you had examined it. When you found him, it would be simple, to the point: why did your father have to die? Take the anger out, cut the emotion, man to man, to the point: why?

When your aunt came out as a believer in front of the whole family, she might as well have been touting her belief in extraterrestrial life. Shortly thereafter, however, things started happening for her. The $6,000 scratch-off ticket she purchased from a Georgia gas station was enough for some families to perk up, as was being cast as an extra in a movie filmed in downtown Birmingham. Like leaves in changing seasons, however, the interest dwindled and, in time, fell dead to earth. How could she, they once again thought, come to find Jesus after losing her son to drugs? Your mother, for good reason, was among her persecutors and was known to roll her eyes behind Aunt Grace's back on more than one occasion.

Now knee-deep in the icy water, you pressed on as if you could hear the hounds. Rocks perhaps previously unseen by man were churned by the thick heels of your business shoes, now cleaned if not ruined. Some kind of smaller fish occasionally circled about before darting off to hidden homes in thin crevices at what must have been an apocalyptic sound and sight. Without notice, the rockface against which you were leaning opened up to a shallow bank, revealing a series of small caves. She had been right. This was where to make your presence known.

"Hello?" you called out in a cracking, weak voice. No response, save for a faint echo. This was a mistake; you had been duped. What if, by chance, your boss or an old friend were fly-fishing at this exact spot? It was not unheard of for residents of Gadsden to converge upon Tennessee for leisure. That would be the end of you; the humiliation would be too great. More likely, the lottery ticket was a stroke of sheer luck; her movie role a product of her pumpkin face and Cheshire smile.

One more time. "Hello!?" you bellowed after convincing yourself that, no, there was not a soul you knew within one hundred miles of where you were standing. Thinking yourself naïve at best, you turned to leave, prepared to put Aunt Grace on trial before the whole family as a liar at the next gathering.

"I've been waiting for you!" he said. "I heard you the first time, but I wanted to hear you call out again with the confidence of faith." He stepped out of the cave and, as if it were routine, bent down like a crouching bird in an inch of water along the bank and skipped a couple of rocks across the river. When he leaned far enough in front of him, the tip of his perfectly triangular beard penetrated the shallows with the intimacy of a kiss. In imitation, you plucked a rock from the shallows as well and haphazardly threw it in the river.

Ask him; ask him.

"You look just like your pictures," you said after sticking your hands in and out of your pockets, not knowing if you, too, should act as casually as he did. He was shiny, his skin and clothing both, a bleached kind of God. You leaned over and retrieved another smooth, flat stone from beneath your feet.

"Yes, that's what they all say, even your Aunt Grace," he replied.

"How did you know that Grace was my aunt? Sorry, dumb question, I–"

"Calm yourself, kid! She wrote to me some time back that her young nephew was planning to swing by."

Climbing these few rungs on the ladder of conversation had been difficult; small talk and any kind of talk, to be frank, had never been your strong suit. Not much had been since it happened, come to think of it. But this was it, the still point of the turning world. You rolled the smooth stone over in your hand, and glitters of small particles glared ever so slightly, like the notes of a far-off orchestra. When you flung the rock, it struck the middle of the river and sank.

How to address this? How did people lead into this kind of a conversation? "Jesus, can you help me?" It was the best you had at the time.

He threw a stone. *Slap slap slap slap slap* it danced across the ripples and came to rest on the opposite bank.

"Do you believe that I can?"

"I have to believe. I have questions; there are things I need to know and something, in particular, I–"

He stood and popped his spine as he leaned backward and stared into the sky he created. It was an afternoon of superb and simplistic beauty, the stillness of nature like the calm of a sleeping newborn. A gust of wind ripped from a high branch a glowing green leaf, which spun until coming to rest upon the clear waters. You were not inclined to be at peace with creation, let alone outside at all. Not since he died anyway. When you asked Aunt Grace where and how she found God, the last thing you were expecting was a map or a plan or a concrete act or even anything as specific as a Bible verse. You had to cut her off as she mournfully compared your quiet, anxious look with that of your father and then needed say nothing when she asked why you wanted to find him. Wasn't it obvious? Why could she not have said something vague to you that day as you poured her coffee? As the grains of sugar were swept away by the churning current she could have simply stated that she tried to be nicer or that glasses are half-full.

"Okay, here's the deal, kid, if you want a memory take a picture 'cause it'll last longer, but if you want answers, I need a ride and a bite to eat. I'm supposed to be in Florida in a week. An Alabama bed and a hot meal or two ought to get me headed in the right direction. Take it or leave it."

Thankfully, Grace had prepared you for this. You consented with a nod, and he ducked into the cave and out again and, before long, the two of you were headed East on I-40. Jesus tapped his fingers repeatedly on the armrest and bridged the small, silent gap between songs with his out-of-tune humming. On occasion, the sun would streak through the windshield just right, and he would make shadow puppets on the back seat that you could only catch glimpses of in the rearview mirror.

"So, what do you do for fun," you asked, "turn the river into wine?"

He gave a small chuckle and rolled his eyes as if to say, "Haven't heard that one before."

More time passed. "So," you spoke up, surprised that you would have to lead the conversation with such routine, "do you, like, know any card tricks or something? I bet you can do some amazing things." You motioned for him to open the glove compartment, and he obliged. Beneath a handful of brown napkins lay a deck of cards. He shuffled them unnecessarily for nearly five minutes.

"Pick a card, any card! I promise not to look!" You reached over and glanced quickly at the six of clubs and slid it back into the deck, which he proceeded to shuffle again. "Prepare to be amazed! Is *this* your card?!" he exclaimed as he drew out the ten of spades.

"No, I'm afraid not," you said.

"Hmmm...let me try again. *This* is your card!" This time, the two of diamonds was thrust into your view.

"No, not it either."

Repeatedly, he failed to draw the correct card. His cheeks were flushed, and he closed the deck and returned it to the glove compartment; the tapping renewed.

"Sorry about that, must be a little rusty. Say, do you want to stop for a bite to eat?" As he asked this he pointed out the window to a billboard that was still too far off to make out. With haste, it approached, an advertisement for the Six of Clubs Cafe, and like lightning, it disappeared into the rearview mirror.

With your mouth agape, you turned to him over and over, careful not to crash the car. "Did you..." you began to say. "What I mean is... was that on purpose?"

"I have no idea what you are talking about," he replied and stared out the passenger window into the passing pines.

As time passed, few words were exchanged. The absolute and sincere amazement at the possibility of the card trick began to fade in your mind and transform into the feeling that there was some other explanation beyond a supernatural one. Your heart rate slowed. What were you doing? Where was the evidence that one could find God, let alone that this man was the carpenter of Nazareth? The tip of the sun landed upon the trees of the horizon and increasingly the light faded away. Thus, the gas light's sudden glow and *ding* were not overlooked nor overheard by either of you.

You had to spit it out. "Why did my father die so young?" For a while, he thought and more than once opened his mouth to answer but relented and stared out the window. The tension packed into the car prompted you to crack all four windows to release some of it back into the nature in which this whole thing started. "He was helping *me* while we were camping, not dealing drugs, not murdering or stealing or raping or cheating like so many who go on living and thriving and wasting money but helping. You killed him, didn't you? I'm the one who disobeyed and climbed up the rock wall; I should've died that day."

The tapping stopped. "Why did *I* die so young?" he replied.

You rolled all the windows down as far as they would go and gripped the wheel, the unlucky victim of your anger. You couldn't speak through that clenched jaw. Why did *you* die so young? If you are who you say you are it's because you couldn't keep your mouth shut in a world of injustice. Better still, you couldn't or didn't want to change the world's injustices. You were innocent and wouldn't speak up? You knew they were coming for you, but you stayed there and prayed? Their hearts were there for the molding like clay and you turned them into stone against you. Were you so desperate for attention that you'd permit your own arrest at the hands of mere men so as to go on trial before Pilate? Maybe that was your plan; when Barabbas was released, it all went wrong, but by then, it was too late, and two days later, your Apostles stole the body from the tomb and staged quite a coup.

Ding.

Less than a mile later, you exited the interstate and parked the car at a gas pump. Jesus stepped out of the vehicle as well and stretched his legs.

"Do you have a few bucks I could borrow?"

You gave him a five.

"Want anything? A lottery ticket?"

You stared into his eyes, an eternity wrapped up within seconds, and shook your head ever so slightly. As he turned to enter the store, his eyes remained locked into yours as long as his neck would allow him. As soon as they snapped apart, you ripped the pump from the gas tank and jumped into the car. He failed to notice as you slammed the door and started the engine and jetted from the parking lot into sudden traffic. When he emerged into the chilly evening with a Diet Coke, he looked about and failed to find you for a few moments. "Come on, come on," you said to the stoplight. When you looked back, he was still glancing around, and you remained as of yet unseen. Still red. Cars darted across the intersection both ways. You leaned forward and saw their stoplights click to yellow. Upon turning your head one last time, your eyes again locked momentarily like two people at a party who are sure they've met. If he had run, he could have caught your car before the light clicked green. As it was, he lifted his drink with a nod as if he knew this would happen and began a stride due south with his thumb sky high.

James 3:1

The school year was young, merely five days old, and yet this was only Mr. Abernathy's second day in the classroom. He was typically not one to lie, but on this Friday morning, he was going to have to find some way to make a new impression, strong yet passionate. This was because on Monday morning, he made the mistake of asking one of his sophomores to "Please sit down, please," as if the fifteen-year-old had the option. The child did not sit, at least at first. Mr. Abernathy asked for his name, and the child said that it was Chuck.

After an obviously meaningless threat of detention, Chuck sat in the closest empty desk and, much like a cat perched atop a bookshelf, began to observe his teacher with more of a curiosity than an interest in learning. Mr. Abernathy proceeded to explain the syllabus while keeping an eye on Chuck who was slipping more and more into a deep sleep. The teacher's impassioned speech about how he was thrilled to communicate the importance and relevance of American History to them did not impress.

The reality was that Mr. Abernathy (Justin to everyone else) had been laid off only three months earlier after two years working in a well-established law firm in Birmingham. He felt unworthy and unfit as a husband and father. The root of these feelings was an insecurity that his wife would thrive in something as subjective as landscape architecture while his knowledge of the law rotted in his mind like fruit on the countertop. His mother was a teacher. It was she who suggested the profession, just as a temporary solution. Justin still remembers her reputation. She was the teacher everyone feared, the one who dropped an assignment a letter grade for using one too many commas or an improper heading. If one was not in the habit of underlining book titles, he might as well register for summer school.

Now that he was standing before them again, he realized why his mother came home most days with the scowl of a drill sergeant. How would he, the new guy, explain these crutches and this hideous leg brace? Three mornings earlier, Mr. Abernathy had to call in a substitute. As the sun rose, he tripped on the open door of his dishwasher while walking backwards through the kitchen, and after a half-twist in the air fell on the large kitchen knife sticking up from the silverware basket like a stalagmite. The blade penetrated his leg just above the knee, cut into his quadriceps tendon, and required surgery to repair. If his day-old reputation with the students were not badly damaged enough it would have been on life support after a story like that. Now, on the Friday morning of his return, as he leaned forward into his crutches, this is the fictional account he relayed to them.

"On Tuesday morning, my elderly neighbor must have seen me from her kitchen window as I walked to my car to go to work. She yelled at me from the garage, 'Justin, Mr. Justin!' I swiftly turned to see her rocking side to side as she hurried in my direction.

"'Please, sir, I need your help today,' she said, and she explained that her plumber had replaced her bathroom vanity and left the old ceramic pedestal leaning against the wall in the garage. She did not want to throw it away but desired to see it recycled or given to a family who needed it. I told her I would be happy to help. As I loaded it into the backseat of my car, a rush of black and gold water flew out of the old faucet and onto the sleeve of my button-down shirt. I tried to ignore the dirty stain after rubbing off what I could on the seat of my car. Though irritated, I drove off.

"Now, there is a thrift store a little off the beaten path on my way to work. I remember passing it by just a few weeks ago as I followed the moving truck that was delivering our things to our new home. Those are roads that I am still unfamiliar with, and I could not remember the name of the store. I was quickly lost. I asked for directions from an elderly man out walking his dog, but he just waved his wrinkly hands in the air and uttered some words no person could ever understand. I drove on. The wet sleeve, now sticking to my skin, was beginning to annoy me to the point of distraction. Out of caution, I tapped the brake a bit as I approached a coming intersection and began to roll up my sleeves. Suddenly, I caught a glimpse of a speeding SUV just as it rammed into my driver-side door. If I had not hit the brakes to adjust my sleeve, I would have slid by just in time.

"A sharp piece of something or other sliced through my left leg. My khaki pants soaked up the blood, and I was in a bit of a state of shock. Before long, I think, a man came to my window, took a look at me, and brought me an old, black t-shirt to press on the wound. After my airbag deflated, I could see that the young girl behind the wheel of the SUV was ghostly white. She spoke with a witness, who proceeded to call for paramedics.

"After exiting my car through the passenger door with difficulty, I limped to the girl to ask if she was okay. She sniffled and nodded. I took the opportunity to take a picture of her car and mine as well as a picture of her. As I was doing so, the sirens of the coming police and paramedics reached our ears. I sat down on the curb and waited in the shade of an old oak.

"The police were the first to land on the scene. They asked me a few questions and said I probably only needed some stitches. Without saying as much, they wanted me to suck it up and move on. When the paramedics arrived shortly after, they were a little nicer but essentially gave the same diagnosis. Why pay the price of an ambulance ride for stitches? Seemed logical to me, though something told me that they were wrong about my leg. Interestingly, however, the girl who had hit me was loaded into the back of the ambulance and driven away despite her having no apparent injuries. Her mother arrived in a panic only a minute too late, and I pointed her in the direction of the ambulance, which I assumed was also the direction of the hospital.

"I was unable to drive and, apart from a lingering officer, was on my own. My wife was over an hour and a half away in Mobile with her mother and our three children for breakfast. My wife texted me the phone number of her aunt, who lives alone in a townhouse near the spot of the accident. I called, and she was willing to pick me up and drive me to the emergency room.

"The drive was awkward. Although I was very thankful for the lift, she had lined the passenger's seat with old towels as if I were bleeding from head to toe. She insisted on staying with me in the hospital until my wife arrived and thus was present when the ER doctor sent a few pictures to an orthopedic surgeon. Only minutes later, a message came back that I needed not only stitches but also surgery on my quadriceps tendon. What a day. Nearly immediately, I was rolled away to the OR preparation area with the aunt by my side.

"My wife finally arrived with our newborn and a thin bouquet of re-gifted lilies from my mother-in-law, who called in sick to her part-time job at a boutique to watch the older two children. What a relief it was to see her! However, the stress that stretched across my wife's face made me feel guilty, almost even responsible for what had happened. As I showed her the pictures of the accident on my phone, the aunt was preparing to leave. Suddenly, she looked over my wife's shoulder and gasped, saying, 'I know her! That's Tabitha!' She recognized the ghostly girl who had run the stop sign.

"She began to explain that Tabitha was the daughter of a close friend. Not only that, but Tabitha was pregnant, which explains why she was loaded into the ambulance that morning. My wife asked the nurse if the girl was in the same hospital and if she and her baby were okay. Within minutes, the nurse returned and told us that, indeed, she was in the hospital for a short time longer. Not only that, but the young mother and unborn child were doing fine. Room 229.

"The aunt informed us that she would stop and see Tabitha on her way out on behalf of the three of us. A bit overwhelmed by the odor, I suggested that she take the lilies to the girl's room as a sign of peace. The aunt thought this to be a beautiful gesture, wished us well, and was off.

"Just as I was being prepared for surgery, the aunt returned, except this time she was teary-eyed and sniffling. My wife comforted her, but she said she did not need it. Tabitha's family, she said, refused to pay for any unnecessary doctor visits when they learned that their seventeen-year-old daughter was pregnant. As such, she had not had an ultrasound to determine the sex of the baby although she was twenty-one weeks gestation. Because of the accident, an emergency ultrasound was ordered. Up to that point Tabitha had known the unborn child to be a girl; she could feel it in her heart, and her name was to be 'Lily.' This morning, however, she received quite a surprise when she learned that the baby was a boy. She took the lilies brought by the aunt as a sign of what the name of the little one ought to be. Tabitha decided to name the baby 'Justin' after me."

At this point in the story, at least four of the young ladies in the sophomore history class were crying. A box of tissues passed between them. The rest of the students, including the young men, were absolutely awestruck at the power of the story. Some laughed, others gasped and whispered among themselves. This was true of all except Chuck, who was sitting back comfortably with arms crossed. His gaze was fixed like marble as if he had not heard a single word. Mr. Abernathy tried to add a closing sentence, something like, "And Tabitha and I have been in touch each day since," but it was unnecessary. He had won them over.

That afternoon after the final bell, Mr. Abernathy packed his things, locked his room, and limped with his crutches down the hall towards the front door. The air was cool, and he belonged. He was a teacher, and a good one at that. He had control, the fruit of power; compromise was for the weak. He had heard that this was the first step in the direction of a successful school year. Take control, his mother had said, and do not smile until Christmas. Only when they are yours can you be theirs. He would come back from the weekend having been given a fresh start.

Mr. Abernathy stopped in the hallway to adjust his leg brace. On his right, the door to another classroom was open, and when he turned to look, his eyes met those of a female teacher whose name he did not yet know. She peered into him through her glasses and stared him up and down before returning to her conversation with a young boy. The greasy-haired student sighed through his scowl. He threw back his head in frustration. The teacher pulled up a chair next to the boy and laid what must have been his paper before them.

Mr. Abernathy pushed through the doors of the school with the confidence of a graduating senior, and the pleasant air warmed him to the bones as he limped across the parking lot. When he reached his car, there was Chuck leaning against it.

"Is this where she hit you?" he asked while pointing to the driver-side door.

"Yes, of course, now please excuse me, Chuck, I

have got—"

"Well, they sure did repair it quickly. Which repair shop did you use? Also," he said as he glanced through the window of the rear door, "I don't see the sink. Did you find time to bring it to the thrift store? What was the name of it again?"

"Chuck, I have a family at home; I don't have time for—"

"Funny how the police department has no record of your accident. My dad's a police officer, you know, and I called him at lunch. He says the only wreck on Tuesday morning between 6:00 and 8:00 was a fender bender between two old ladies in a parking lot."

"Well, I respect your father and what he does for a living but—"

"And ain't it strange that no one in our school knows anyone in this town with the name of Tabitha? There's only two high schools in this city, but I guess you wouldn't know that, being from Birmingham."

Mr. Abernathy opened his mouth to defend himself, but the words got stuck in his throat. Chuck drew a few steps closer, shook his teacher's hand, and asked for an extension for that weekend's homework assignment. Mr. Abernathy acquiesced, just this once.

Chuck's mother honked her car horn and threw up her hands from the road where she had stopped only seconds earlier. The sophomore sped off in her direction. He turned only to wave

goodbye before flinging his backpack to the floor
and hopping into the front seat.

The Grove

As he was layered with the heavy rope, Dillon struggled to convince himself that the rumors about the farmer were fabricated.

When John finished, he tried to get through to Dillon about the importance of grades and handed him an amateur map drawn up on a sheet of paper ripped from a notebook.

Dillon had to force it into the pocket of the jeans he was wearing, which only a year ago fit like a glove. He tried to explain to John that the reason for his low GPA last year was that the history professor hated him; he had even, thanks to Janie, earned a 'B' in Literature. It was no use. On his way out, Dillon was told to send in Red, the only other sophomore with grades below the tolerable threshold.

At the sight of the rope, Dillon was bombarded with jeers and textbooks from all of the brothers but Joey, his roommate for the upcoming year. Dillon rubbed his fingers through his patchwork beard and pretended to glory in the dishonor of the responsibility he had been handed.

Red let out a sigh of relief. "Oh, thank God!" he said beneath the baseball cap that was as much a part of his head as his auburn hair. He slapped Dillon on the back and opened John's door. "You're not scared, are you?" Red asked rhetorically before shutting himself in.

Dillon shot him a glance and tried to spin his fear into revel; there was something exciting about now knowing the exact route to the creek, a swimming hole, the location of which was known campus-wide to only a handful. All passengers, even fraternity members, were blindfolded until they arrived. The lowest GPA of the freshmen class was given the duty of driver from start to finish of the sophomore year. This meant not only staying sober but also an immediate drive to the creek to clear the path of summer's brush and to hang up the rope swing. Dillon, Joey, and Red made a pact that no matter who was punished, the other two would help out with the duties of the day.

Joey stood nearby. "Sure as hell glad it's not me," he said as a few freshmen behind him practiced the fraternity handshake. They joined their right hands, tucked in their ring fingers, and gripped tightly twice before letting go. They perked up their ears to hear more about Dillon's assignment.

Dillon knew exactly what Joey was thinking. Although few knew the specific location, most had an idea that it required driving on the property of the irascible farmer Michael Cordia. The terrible old man, it was said, hated college students, especially those who trespassed on his land.

"Old Cordia once dug a pit and trapped a truck like an animal," Joey said louder than usual so that the freshmen could be brought into the fold. "The passengers climbed out and ran, but by the time the tow truck arrived, it was buried as if nothing had happened. Their parents were furious, but there was nothing they could do."

"Maybe that's true," said a nearby senior, "but that wasn't half as bad as the group that was tortured in his basement before waking up on the side of the road as the sun was rising the next day. That's why he's called Misery Cordia."

Dillon blindfolded Joey and Red and herded the pair into his truck. For miles they drove away from campus down County Road 83. Row after row of pecan trees stretched across countless acres to the left. On the right, pop-up neighborhoods dotted the landscape. Dillon glanced back and forth between the map and the odometer. They were getting close. John's map bounced up and down on his knee and indicated a turn at any moment. The red clay road, hidden by thick brush, was suddenly only yards away, and Dillon turned sharply onto it off of the highway. Joey was thrown into Red's lap. Clumps of mud showered the vehicle like raindrops. Dillon's truly urban truck had a rural façade and was not accustomed to driving on anything other than concrete. Red held Joey in a tight grip.

"Oh, Joey, I didn't know you loved me *that*

much!" Red said.

Joey simply shuffled back to his side of the truck; his nerves were clearly on edge, a condition Dillon was not in this moment immune to either. He pressed the gas in his white Chevy, and the exhaust roared. Near the end of the road, a cautious turn through a small space in the foliage landed them on the property of the old farmer. Dillon sighed. He had not been this nervous since he first saw Janie about this time last year. The humiliation of failing now was the only thought worse than physical torture in the basement of Misery Cordia.

"Light me up when you got a second," Red said. A cigarette hung from his lips.

Dillon reached into the backseat and put his lighter to the tip. "Didn't you just smoke one before we left?" Dillon asked as he rolled down the windows.

"You sound just like my mom," Red said. "And, no, that ain't a compliment."

For nearly a mile, Dillon's truck hugged a line of trees on the right of the old man's land. This ended abruptly against a field of corn. Dillon parked and turned the map over in his hands because the last thing he wanted was to end up on Cordia's doorstep. Red's impatience became palpable. He drummed on the back of the seat in front of him and hummed a song so out of tune that it rivaled a fork across a plate. The truck crept along and wove until it was wedged between two rows of pecan trees, which hung over the truck like giants. Wisteria vines reached low like long fingers as if to grab them. After a few minutes of driving, the line of trees came to an end, and the truck was parked face to face with a pine forest. Dillon tucked his vehicle as well as he could in the corner of the property.

"You can take your blindfolds off," Dillon said. He flung open the door and jumped out of the truck. He began to flick drops of red clay off of the frame. The expensive mud tires were nearly half Dillon's height, and he stepped on one to inspect the roof of the truck for scratches from the vines.

Joey cautiously stepped from the vehicle and hid behind a pine tree. "Thank God we're here," he said. "You drive like a maniac." For such a large person, Joey had a soft heart, evidenced by his dedication to the fraternity charity. After his efforts volunteering last year, Joey was made the philanthropy chair this morning by the president. Dillon could have sworn that he even saw Joey praying once or twice. Like a parent on the playground, he was the fraternity's necessary interloper. His commitment to save his first sip of alcohol for his twenty-first birthday lasted less than a month into their freshman year, but his attendance record was a boost for the class average. He asked permission, not forgiveness, and because they did not have it, he hid behind a tree.

Red set his lit cigarette on the hood. It was hard

to believe that this young man was the most reserved pledge of their freshmen class. He came from out of state, and everything that comes with pledge life, from duties to nicknames and insults to pranks, emboldened him. The dam was cracked, and the firecracker personality that had percolated for however many years could now be silenced only by sleep or heavy doses of alcohol. "That truck's only going to get dirty on the way back," Red said. "Let's just hurry up and get this path cleared out."

Dillon removed the rope and two machetes from a silver toolbox in the bed of the truck, and the three of them took turns hacking at the overgrown vines and branches. After not very much work, the path opened into a clearing. The swimming hole lay before them just as they remembered it. The three of them stopped at the edge of the still water and exchanged smiles. Dillon did not know how long they had reminisced before Red pushed him and Joey in.

If the water had not been so refreshing, Dillon would have been frustrated. Although a bit embarrassed by his weight, he removed his soaked shirt and sucked in his gut. The freshman fifteen had ballooned into the freshman forty, and after the weight gain, hiding it as much as possible was now a habit. This was quite a fall from grace for the former decathlete. After roughly half an hour, the three of them tied up the rope swing and lay in the sun to dry off. Red spoke of his summer job filling boats with gasoline and cleaning fish at a marina back home. "I met a girl there too, but I broke it off with her pretty quick," he said. "I wouldn't want to be whipped like Dillon over here."

"Shut up, Red," Dillon shot back. "I barely talked to Janie all summer, so lay off." This was a lie. The truth, which he hid from the brothers like his gut, was that he loved her; it was only a question of how much. She was cute but nerdy, the type that was quick to answer questions in freshman literature because she actually read the material. One day, he slipped in line behind her at the coffee shop on campus, and when she hesitated for only a moment, he paid for hers and his together. This became their date, so that three days a week, they could get to know one another under the guise of studying. Janie despised fraternities but admitted that Dillon was not too bad for a frat boy. She was a local girl. Her mother, like her grandmother had for decades, volunteered all of her free time at the Methodist Church not far from campus and had been mistaken for the pastor's wife more than once. "I want to be just like my grandmother," Janie told Dillon. "A table filled with children, unconditional love, and asking nothing in return." He had not called her since he returned to town for the semester, but that morning, he had invited her by text message to the house's party that night. When they finally did speak, he would blame his laziness on fraternity duties.

"Well, it looks like I pushed the right button!" Red said. "It takes a special insult to shut you up for a while. We'd better get out of here to make the meeting tonight."

The trio returned to the white truck, spotted red as if diseased, and began the drive back to the fraternity house. Every now and again on Cordia's land a tree had been felled, perhaps from disease or fruitlessness. With a *crack* something struck the windshield. Dillon hit the brakes after cussing and got out to examine the damage on the otherwise healthy vehicle. He rubbed his fingers over the fracture in the glass, branches of which radiated in all directions.

"Had to have been a pecan," Red said. "That's only going to spread and won't be cheap to fix either." He flicked his cigarette out of the window and lit another.

"You're not supposed to be looking, Red," Dillon said, though he was more concerned about the windshield. "How could a pecan make a crack like this?" he wondered out loud. "I know they're hard and everything, but—"

"It must have fallen from pretty high up," Red interrupted. "Listen, the question is what to do about it. If I were you, I wouldn't let the old man get away with this. I don't know where we are, but we ought to find his driveway and demand he pay for it. I'm sure his trees lean over the highway every so often, so why not say we were just driving down the road when a pecan fell from one of his branches?"

As Joey rattled on about why every part of this idea was terrible and foolish, Dillon took it seriously. If he did it, then it would be he and not Cordia who would be the subject of stories for years to come.

"Fine, let's go," Dillon said, eager to redeem the embarrassment of his grades. "What can he do but say 'no'?" He pulled onto the highway, and before long, a small black mailbox signaled the beginning of an otherwise inconspicuous driveway.

"I heard he has a gun," Joey said from the backseat with a stutter. "Probably more than one, and pit bulls too. If we don't get out of here, we'll—"

"Shut up, you coward!" Red snapped. "He ain't going to shoot us. Even if he did, I heard Janie is studying to be a nurse."

Dillon slammed the brakes, and Red was jolted forward. His face slammed into the seat in front of him.

"We're here," Dillon said. "You can take your blindfolds off."

The old farmer's wooden home was a two-story with a few stairs leading to a covered porch. A long hose stretched like a snake from the back of the house and across the driveway of oyster shells to a small vegetable garden nearby. The white banisters were splattered with black mold and needed cleaning, like much of the exterior. To their right, a scrawny farmhand sat shirtless on a lawn mower. He was staring into his phone, to which the headphones across his scalp were connected. The glory of the imminent meeting placed a hand on Dillon's back and ushered him forward and up the steps. As he lifted his fist to knock, Dillon was surprised by a sudden desire not only for Cordia to answer the door but also to invite him in. His knuckles landed on the door three times. The footsteps that approached the threshold were thick and methodical, as if calculated.

"Who is it?" roared a raspy voice.

"My name's Dillon, Dillon Mickelson," the young man said in return. "I'm a student at A&M."

The door cracked open only enough to permit Cordia's clouded eye to peer through. It scrutinized everything before it as if the very air Dillon breathed were suspicious. The dense eye, cradled by thick, tan wrinkles, finally settled on Dillon's face and thrust into him more a sense of awe than fear.

"What do you want?" the old man said.

For the sake of the audience at his back, Dillon was bold. "Well, sir, a pecan from your grove struck my truck as we were driving down County Road 83. A few of your branches hang over the highway, if you didn't know that already."

For a minute, the eye did little but stare and blink. The hidden mouth then let out a slow, loud cackle as the door was torn open. The old man leaned with both arms on a cane. If Dillon were invited in, he would have tripped over the right leg stuck out straight as an arrow.

"Son, when I was your age, before I built this home with my bare hands, I was gettin' shot at. You realize that?"

"Um, no, sir," Dillon said with a nervous chuckle, and for a moment, he considered whether or not the farmer had once been a gang member or a drug dealer.

"Answer me this, son," Cordia said. "Have you-"

A woman's voice from upstairs broke in. "Who is that, Michael?"

Cordia turned. "Just a minute, Doris, a minute!" he yelled. "We have a few young visitors from the university." He returned his attention to Dillon. "I'm sorry, son, but have you studied the war, that is, World War II?"

Doris called from upstairs yet again, saying, "Aren't you going to invite them in? Don't be rude, and don't bore them with your old stories."

"Just a minute, honey!" the old man said. After waiting a moment to ensure there was no reply, he said to Dillon, "Now answer my question. What do you know about the war?"

Dillon glanced over his shoulder for help but received none. Okay, he thought, World War II. That means there were at least two world wars. It was coming back. He had it; he had it!

"That was when Franz Ferdinand was killed"" Dillon said with confidence. "I think that's right,

right?"

Cordia let out a deep sigh. "Son," he said, "I am not fixing your windshield. Turn around and go home. If you want to swim in the creek, I advise you go about it all legally or not at all." He took a step across the threshold and yelled to the distracted farmhand on the tractor, "Back to work, Rick!" His order was unheard. Cordia descended the stairs between the brothers and threw a rock from the garden bed with pinpoint accuracy into the body of the farmhand motionlessly straddling the tractor. "Back to work!"

Rick threw back his head in frustration and shoved the phone into the pocket of his khaki shorts. "Oh, whatever you say, sir!" he said. He throttled the engine.

✠

After the fraternity meeting that evening, the happenings of the afternoon spread among the brothers. Although Dillon insisted on his courage throughout the meeting with Misery Cordia, Red imitated Dillon's look of fear as the door in front of the cloudy eye was flung open. All in all, the brothers admired Dillon, but a handful nudged him little by little to get even.

"You ain't got those mud tires for nothing!" Red said. "Why don't we put them to good use tonight?"

Dillon shot him a look across the dinner table. "No way."

"What, afraid your truck will get a little dirty? That's what pledges are for, remember!"

"No, it's not worth it. I don't want any more trouble," Dillon said. In something of an attempt to change the subject, Dillon asked some of the other brothers about World War II and why his answer had not satisfied the farmer.

Red did not take the bait and instead pushed out his chair and stood on top of it like a step stool. He cupped his hands around his mouth like a megaphone. "Attention everyone, Dillon is too scared to—"

Dillon reached across the table and pulled him down and close to his own face. "Fine!" he said. "No one but Joey, and I mean absolutely no one, can know about it or come with us, got it?"

"Got it, I got it," Red said through his yellow teeth. "We'll meet at your truck in half an hour."

✠

That night, the three returned to the property. Joey's knees bobbed up and down against the back of the driver's seat. Once deep into the grove, Dillon let them take off the blindfolds. A full moon illuminated the night, and its rays pierced a few of the thick branches like silver spears.

"We have got to make this quick," Dillon said. "Janie is coming over to the house tonight when the band starts."

"I thought you said she hated fraternities," Joey said. "Why would she want to come over to our house, and while we're at it, why are we even here right now; why did I agree to this? Let's get out of here while we got the chance."

Red punched him in the shoulder and called him a wimp. "Dillon, let's get on with it! It's a little bright for my liking, and besides, we do not want to keep Janie waiting."

The truck roared like a lion when Dillon slammed the accelerator. They weaved in and out and all around the arching giants and left deep tracks in the wet earth. Mud and grass were thrown into the air behind them. Joey buried his face in his hands, and Red screamed with excitement. Dillon had never done anything like this, but it gave him a thrill he had rarely felt. What Janie might think, what his parents might say if they heard, was irrelevant. They drew near the path to the creek and turned around; at least two of them had their minds set on doing more damage. After a couple more minutes, they neared the end of the cornfield on what was to them the left side of the property.

"What's that?" Dillon asked. When they were fifty feet away, they could see it more clearly. A vacant tractor was parked in the middle of their path. Dillon pressed the brake with a soft foot.

Joey broke the silence. "That wasn't here before, was it?"

Red strained his eyes and leaned over Joey to get a better look. "Sure it was; we just didn't notice it before. I think I remember seeing it. Don't you, Dillon?"

Dillon shook his head and eased his foot off of the brake. Like a postman, he rolled down the window and reached his hand out towards the tractor, placing his hand upon the hood. He gasped and turned to his friends. "It's warm," he said. "How could it be warm?"

From behind a pecan tree, the barrel of a shotgun emerged, followed by the limping body of the man who held it. Like an old dog, he shuffled to a spot directly in front of the truck. Joey ducked and covered his head with his arms and screamed something about having told them so. Red said to run him over because they had a right to if their lives were threatened. Dillon shifted into reverse and hit the gas, but the tires only spun on their axles and churned-up mud like fireworks.

"Stop trying to be nice and go!" Red screamed.

The wheels spun. Cordia raised the gun. Red ducked beside Joey as Dillon put up his hands as if to surrender, remembering what the old man had said about being shot at in his youth. Before he closed his eyes, Dillon saw a wry smile come across the old face as the gun settled on his shoulder. The moment after the weapon was fired felt like an eternity. However, no glass shattered. No one screamed or bled. Dillon cracked open his eyes like peanuts.

Pecans and branches rained down like hail, rattling the truck with a chorus of cracks and thuds. The antenna was snapped. Cordia let out a ringing cackle and fired into the tree again with the same effect on the truck. Through the open window he shouted at Dillon, "Son, just like I told you this afternoon, turn around!" He reloaded. "Your truck's in the way of my harvest! Can't you see I'm out to farm? Turn around!" He fired into the tree twice more.

Now that Cordia had walked to one side of the path, Dillon thrust the truck into drive and accelerated steadily to dislodge the tires. He drove around the farmer as another shot was fired. More pecans landed like buckshot, and a thick branch slammed into the bed and shattered a brake light. Dillon hit the gas and swiped a tree with his side mirror, which broke off and rolled to the feet of Cordia. Dillon accelerated as a final blast from the gun trumpeted a closing onslaught of pecans and branches. He clenched his fists, and no one said a word until the bruised vehicle parked at the fraternity house.

✠

Janie's presence at the party that night—her first visit to the fraternity house—was both refreshing and awkward. She was a relief from his brothers, but Dillon could tell that she knew that there was something about the evening that hung over him like a rain cloud. He did not want to talk about it, he said. To top it all off, Dillon found out that Janie did not dance and, soon after, that she despised the band and still did not drink. He wrestled all night with the question of how and why he was attracted to her. He did know that it was powerful and, by the way she clung to him that evening, mutual as well.

Dillon, however, did drink, and often too much. This night was no exception, and he needed it after what had happened to his truck. A few drinks in, he still refused to tell Janie what had happened but begged her not to go into the parking lot.

✠

Like dual alarm clocks, the snoring and the smell jolted Dillon out of bed and to his feet. He was shirtless but had slept in his jeans. Joey either fell off of his bed or drank too much to notice the difference, but either way his roommate was curled up with Dillon's quilt on the floor between their beds. Dillon wondered if Janie had seen him to bed or if she had had enough of him before that. What did she think when she saw him like that? He was embarrassed that he could not remember, and he was absolutely sure that the relationship had come to a cold end until he saw the note written in large letters on the nightstand:

"I received some bad news tonight. My grandmother passed away suddenly before she went to sleep this evening. I am sorry I had to leave early. I had fun, I promise."

Dillon let out a sigh. Poor girl. He washed his face in the bathroom and looked at himself in the mirror. His cheeks were round. He glanced over his shoulder to make sure Joey was still asleep and flexed his muscles. They were not there.

Dillon ripped a shirt off of the floor and threw it over his body. It was only 9 a.m. and quiet as usual for a Saturday morning in the fraternity house. Dillon went downstairs and found John poring over the previous day's mail at the kitchen table. He looked up over his reading glasses and said, "Good morning, sunshine! I heard about your run-in last night with Cordia, tough luck. I guess all the rumors about the old man must be true, huh?"

How did he know? "Well he's got another thing coming," Dillon said as if he meant it.

John kept his head down and fingered through the letters. "Your girl was cute last night. Janie, right? Kind of nerdy, though, don't you think?"

"Yeah, well, I think I'll break it off with her," Dillon lied.

"Anyway, this is probably one of the last things you want to hear, but you're up for another trip to the creek today. Between my SUV and your truck, we ought to be able to carry all of the seniors; they've been looking forward to it. You should know the route well enough now, having been there twice and all." Before Dillon could interject about the damage to his truck, John said that they would throw a few bucks his way to help with repairs. "Besides, I don't think your insurance company is going to believe there was a hailstorm last night!"

✠

Later that day on the way to the creek, Dillon's phone buzzed inside the cup holder. Janie was calling. Red was in the front seat.

"Who's that?" he asked.

"Just my mom. I'll call her back later."

During his swim at the creek, Dillon received a text message: "Why won't you answer my calls?" And another an hour later: "Do you care about me or not?"

He replied, "Yes," but that was all she needed to know. She did not control him; they were not engaged, not to mention he had never even called her his girlfriend. It was what she thought of him versus dozens of others, most importantly those brothers he lived with. A reputation is a terrible thing to waste. A few hours later, the caravan departed from the creek. Near the cornfield, the lazy farmhand was bending low over the sprinklers. Dillon had an idea and he rolled down his window.

"Rick," he called. "Hey, Rick!" Like a deer, the farmhand stood up straight and stared at them, probably more curious about the attention than why trucks traipsed across his master's property. Although John kept driving, Dillon stopped nearby and slipped Rick a twenty-dollar bill. "Tomorrow night," Dillon commanded, "leave an upstairs window open in Cordia's home and a ladder leaning against the roof. Understand? If you do it, you can expect more where this came from."

For a moment, Rick stared into him as if searching for the meaning of it all. His face was filthy and bits of grass were stuck in his hair. Suspicious, the farmhand took the bill from Dillon with his green hand, pocketed the money, and nodded. He went back to work without saying a word.

✠

Two nights later, Dillon recruited Joey to drop him and Red off at the end of Cordia's driveway. As they drove down County Road 83, Janie texted again: "I needed you yesterday. I needed you today." Regarding this relationship, Dillon held firm. If she wanted him that badly, then she could sit on it and wait a while and see how she felt then.

Joey slowed to a stop on the quiet highway, let the two out and said he'd be waiting for their phone call down the road. As Dillon and Red walked up the long driveway, it was clear from quite a distance, that the Cordia's home was well-lit. After a few paces, it was Red who broke the silence. "Okay, now will you tell me your plan?"

Another message came from Janie: "I still need you tonight. Are you there? Please call!"

Dillon shoved his phone into his pocket and slowed as if to turn around. After a deep breath, he decided against it and answered Red's question. "You are going to wait behind a tree at the back of the house while I put that long garden hose of his through the open upstairs window." Dillon paused for a gulp. "When you see me do that, run to the spigot and turn on the water. Then, we'll run for our lives."

Red rubbed his hands together. "If John knew you were doing *that*, there's no way he would help you pay for that truck of yours. On the other hand, if the brothers found out you came this far only to fail..."

The oyster shells crunched beneath their feet. The bright home shined like a torch amidst the dark groves. Like two nights previous, the moon was at its brightest, which lit the many cars that lined the driveway on both sides.

Dillon started to stutter. "No, no, not tonight, there are too many people here."

"It has to be tonight!" Red said. He grabbed Dillon's shoulders and turned him back towards the house. "If he is distracted by visitors, it only makes it easier."

Dillon saw the truth in this and ran from tree to tree on the right as Red swung around the home on the opposite side. There, at the end of the structure, was the ladder propped against the house as instructed. Dillon grabbed the hose and climbed to the roof, the angle of which was sharper than expected. As Dillon leaped onto the shingles, they scraped his knees, and the ladder flew backwards flat to the earth. Did anyone inside see it? Did Red? Dillon crawled to the first window. Locked. The next was locked as well. He crawled to the third and yanked upwards. The old window screamed like a stopping train as it opened. Dillon froze with the hose gripped in both palms, and he looked out into the grove. Red waved him on from behind a pecan tree, but before he could sneak across the yard to reposition the ladder, the back door opened. Three men walked out to smoke cigarettes.

The fifteen minutes that Dillon was frozen on the roof seemed like hours. The men laughed about old memories, from the trouble they were in as children to the forgiving hands of their parents. Their mother's strawberry cake was the best. Surely the recipe was written down somewhere. None of them seemed to notice the hose ascending through the air. Dillon held it perfectly still. Two of the men stomped out their cigarettes and went inside. The one who remained was very large and balding, and as he leaned back against the railing, he sobbed like a small child between puffs. Why was this grown man crying? After the cigarette was finished, he wiped his eyes and turned around to ascend the stairs. He stopped suddenly and pivoted slightly to the left. Dillon could not see what he did with his eyes. He followed the other two inside after grinding his own cigarette into the wood floor.

Dillon turned and thrust the hose into the window and shouted to Red to get the ladder. Only seconds later, the fraternity brother fled as fast as he could in the opposite direction into the dark, sprawling groves. The back door opened. Dillon saw the light from their flashlights before he saw the men themselves. He leapt into the house, but like an anchor rope, the hose slipped out and fell to the ground. The room was an old bedroom, but if he were to hide here or anywhere upstairs for that matter, he was sure to be trapped. Dillon sprinted for the stairs and rode the banister to the first floor. They were coming; their lights flashed through the window from the outside. Footsteps thumped across a nearby room in his direction. Dillon opened the nearest door and closed it behind him. More stairs descended to the basement.

He went down, and like a scared kitten, Dillon huddled behind the washing machine in the back corner. Cobwebs became tangled in his hair. He reached around in the dark for something he could use as a weapon, but there was nothing within reach. The instruments of torture were probably close by. Suddenly, the door at the top of the stairs was flung open. The sudden light cast away the thick darkness and penetrated every crevice. The sharp rap of a cane preceded each thick step as the old figure descended down into the basement of the home he had built.

Dillon's hands clenched into fists; there was nowhere left to run. The footsteps reached the bottom of the stairs just as Dillon's phone vibrated in his pocket. As he pulled it out, his gut fell over the top of his belt buckle. Again and again he tried to pull in his stomach, but over and over it slipped out. Janie was calling, probably now for the last time. Who was he? Was there really any use in fighting the old man or what he had gotten himself into? Dillon went to his knees and relaxed his muscles. His parents, let alone Janie, would be ashamed. He turned to face the owner of the home.

Dillon's clenched fists unraveled like blooming flowers, and tears fell down his cheeks. With every quiet sob, his stomach bounced. Dillon imagined himself to be nothing but a pitiful creature in need of a mercy killing beneath the gaze of Misery Cordia. His eyes were swollen, and like a beggar, his hands lay open. The old man reached low with his wrinkled hands and snatched at Dillon's earlobe as if it were a threat to fly away. He was pulled slowly and with sharp tugs to the top of the steps where he expected, at worst, the police and, at best, a mob of angry men to be waiting for him.

"Please, have mercy," Dillon said. "Please, please, have mercy." He was led into the kitchen, where the farmer let go of his throbbing ear.

The old man looked him in the eyes and said, "There's no such thing as mercy without justice."

"Why can't you just let me go?"

The farmer for a moment said nothing, but with his eyes, demanded of Dillon a certain introspection. "Would you rather only justice?"

More tears flowed before Dillon whispered, "I choose mercy too." He wondered if his own eyes were at that moment more clouded than Cordia's. "I am sorry. I am so, so sorry."

"Follow me," the farmer said. He limped down

the hallway and, for the first time, Dillon obeyed.

The living room was full of people, and there in the middle of a red sofa, squeezed between what must have been her parents, sat Janie. Dillon's swollen eyes met hers, but she lowered her distraught face. He wanted to reach out to her, to comfort her, and then it clicked: Doris was her grandmother, the funeral was tomorrow. Was it too late to beg for mercy from her as well?

"As you're all aware," Cordia said, "Willoughby was Doris' favorite cat and has been missing since her passing. Dillon here, such a nice young man, did not spot her on the roof nor in the basement, did you, son?"

Dillon stiffened like a board and cleared his throat. "No, sir."

"And you will leave no stone unturned until he turns up, will you?"

Dillon stared at the audience, and they, apart from Janie, stared back. His tongue, which had been so quick to speak for most of his life, was dried to the roof of his mouth. "No, sir, I will not."

"Since Willoughby was accustomed to eating a large breakfast between 5:00 and 5:30, I am sure that Dillon will be back first thing in the morning before the funeral to see if the poor thing turns up. Before he slipped away, however, Dillon wanted to say a few words."

Did he mean 5:00 a.m.? He strained to remember a time he was up that early in recent memory. "Uh," he muttered, "good evening."

A few mourners returned the greeting, but Janie stared at her shoes. Dillon shifted his weight and searched for words. "I, um, I'm sorry if I scared any of you while I was on the roof. I didn't mean to. I think that Mrs. Cordia was a good woman, a lovely woman."

Dillon did not know from where within him that statement came, but it was enough to stir Janie to finally glance up at him. The brown eyes behind the black glasses were like a pool he could fall into.

"Well, by that, I mean that I know she was lovely. I never met her, but someone very special to me looked up to Mrs. Cordia and tried to be like her." Dillon pulled from within him a sincerity that he had never used and peered around the room. "If this young woman has succeeded in imitating her grandmother, then I know first-hand that the late Mrs. Cordia was a woman of honor, love, and generosity." Now staring straight into the eyes he loved, he finished by saying, "I am so sorry for your loss. Good evening, everyone." He turned to leave and shook the widower's hand.

The old man walked him to the door and said so that everyone could hear, "Goodbye, Dillon, and thank you! I will see you first thing in the morning then, and I have confidence that you will accept my offer to take the place of Rick, who, I am sad to announce, resigned from working under my care only this afternoon. We can start slow, Dillon. Is 6:00 next Saturday morning okay with you, or is that too late of a start for an up-and-coming farmhand like yourself?"

Janie cupped her hand over her mouth to shield the laughter. Dillon's heart leapt upon seeing just the hint of a smirk behind her small hands. The bald man from outside comforted her as if her tears were those of sorrow.

"No, sir," Dillon said.

"Fantastic, son, and I will see you tomorrow and Saturday morning first thing. Before you leave, here is a twenty dollar advance!" Cordia searched the pockets of his jacket with his wrinkled hands and pulled out the same bill that Dillon had slipped Rick earlier. When Dillon reached for it, Cordia clenched his hand tight, tucked in his ring finger, gripped twice, and let go. Dillon's heart and head beat and spun with such rapidity that he could hardly take it all in. In a daze, he was pushed to the porch and handed the broken mirror from his truck. Dillon received it with both hands as if it were a gift.

"First thing you should learn about me, Dillon, is that I was a damn good shot in the war." Cordia picked up another rock from the garden bed and slung it across the yard, striking and shattering a clay pot. "Still got it!" he said.

Dillon, mouth agape, descended the steps of the porch and began to stumble as if drunk down the driveway towards the main road. Mr. Cordia called after him to remind him to eat breakfast. Dillon took deep breaths and cleared his head.

The pace of his heart returned to normal.

After the front door closed, Red sprinted from the darkness and began to question Dillon with his quick mouth. "Tell me what happened!" A lit cigarette glowed between his fingers. "Are you going to jail? Were you tortured? Oh, God knows I tried to help, but when they came out with those flashlights I had no choice but to run away. This ain't the end; we can still get him back! Hey, why are you crying?"

Dillon did not answer because he was preoccupied. The light from his phone illuminated his face as he texted Janie: "Forgive me?"

"Are you listening to me? What was it like in there? What happened?"

Dillon stopped. He turned and stared at his peer, truly seeing him for what felt like the first time. Red's entire face was cast in darkness because of his cap. Dillon handed him the broken mirror and read the incoming message on his phone.

"Liberating," Dillon said through a smile before turning around and leaving Red behind him.

Requiescat in Pace

Your Excellency,

It has fallen upon me by the providence of God to relay to you the circumstances regarding the truly maleficent robbery of the grave of the late Father John Doyle. As you are well aware, not only was there a theft from the coffin but also a horrific dismemberment of the body itself. The curiosities of this heinous act I am at the moment keeping as a secret and hidden from the frenzy of the media, the trucks of which, with their satellites pointed skyward remain parked outside the rectory. Many have crossed themselves at the door, purporting to be worshippers.

Allow me to recount those facts as printed in the paper this morning that are indeed true. In the early morning of February 21st, while the night was cold and the darkness thick, the coffin of Father Doyle was unearthed and burglarized. Two men were responsible for the act, one of whom, Mr. Robert Cobb, is as of now recovering from an unsuccessful tongue transplant surgery at Baptist Hospital. I believe that, once mended, other rehabilitations of much greater urgency will commence without hesitation. The other culprit, Mr. Brooks Dawkins, is as of yet on the loose. As I understand it, however, the tip line established for the purposes of his capture has had little time to rest.

The reason I am penning this letter to Your Excellency is twofold. First, and less importantly, I can now testify truthfully that Dawkins is not, in fact, guilty of two of the crimes that he is suspected to have committed. Is he, on the other hand, a criminal, guilty of offenses against the law and against God? Without question this is the case, and I pray that if he does not willingly surrender, that he would be captured and brought to justice. Second, and of much greater significance, I believe the truth of that terrible day to be of particular interest to our historic diocese and the glory of God. This I will unfold.

At around eleven AM on that day, Mrs. Sandra Juniper, a parishioner of ours, approached the doors of the church in hopes of lighting a candle before Our Lady in hopes of furthering the cause to which our parish has so diligently devoted itself over these last few years. This is her daily custom. What awaited her at the door was a man huddled in the fetal position. Mrs. Juniper of all Catholics has a heart of pure gold. She inquired as to his needs. Food? Water? Shelter? Clothing? Money? He said nothing, and she reached down to him in the posture of our Lord. Her hand rested on the gruff shoulder.

The man rolled over like a log to face her and sat up on his elbow. His mouth was full of blood. He could not speak, and as it dribbled from his lips and down his beard and over his clothing, he made the Sign of the Cross and pointed to his collar. Mrs. Juniper, obviously horrified, retrieved me from the rectory. This man was, as you now know, Mr. Cobb.

As Mrs. Juniper called for an ambulance, I attempted to pray over this helpless man, but he would not allow me. He swatted at my hands. With both fists, he gripped my shirt and pulled my face intimately close to his. He struggled to utter a single word. Over and over, he spit out the blood and repeated the syllables. It was as if his life depended upon my understanding, but I could not decipher it.

"Conscience?"

He shook his head. More blood dripped to the marble steps.

"Regression?   Conditional?   Admission? Additional?" Again, no.

Perhaps he was telling me his name. "Connor? Andrew? Ferguson? Michael? Johnson?" All incorrect. He waved his arms about and pointed over his shoulder. From down the road, the ambulance approached with rapid speed; I was running out of time.

When I saw the penance in his eyes and followed the line painted by his pointing finger through the church doors, I thought for a moment and muttered, "Confession?" At this he lit up, but before he could mumble his sins, the paramedics arrived and placed him on a stretcher. I prayed a general prayer of absolution over the rolling body. My intention was to visit this man with the stole draped over my shoulders in the very near future.

The investigator was a brusque man, carrying on his face the weight of justice. I answered his questions as well as I could as his men roped off the church steps. He cared not that Cobb needed confession. Bulbs flashed and news cameras rolled. At long last, the mania subsided, and our historic church was returned to me. The reporters were given further instruction by the officers, all of whom departed silent and serene.

It was when the investigator knocked on the rectory door later that afternoon that I learned two important things about Mr. Cobb: he was addicted to methamphetamine, which did not surprise me, and that evidence placed him at the scene of a grave robbery from that morning. This was my first word of the incident, which saddened me to the point of grief. The misery that I had first felt upon the death of my grandfather as a young boy resurrected within me like a dormant virus. I leaned against the doorframe. The accomplice, Mr. Dawkins, was as of yet on the loose. The two of them had committed similar crimes across state lines.

"A warrant is being issued for his arrest for not only the assault on Cobb and the burglary, but also for the theft of body parts with the intent to sell," the investigator said as he lifted his hat to his head. "And one more thing. You may want to park your car down the street if you plan on going anywhere."

"What do you mean?" I asked.

"When the media comes back, it won't just be the locals." He departed.

Sleep did not welcome me that evening. I stumbled about, unable to finish my meal. With a prayer card in my shaking hand, I carried out a vigil in the church through the night. Within me, grief and peace held hands as if I did not have to choose between the two.

The following afternoon, this afternoon, I entered the confessional for our parish's weekly scheduled penance when, to my surprise and horror, I discovered two items of note. The first was not truly one item but many, a stack of prayer cards upon which had been scribbled a story. There were as many as thirty, containing sentences such as, "Switched them out," and "Banged my head." Cobb had been here first. I have put together the dozens of little clues into the following narrative, which, while perhaps imperfect, is certainly the approximate truth of that awful morning.

Cobb and Dawkins are the latest in a series of thieves to unearth the dead in order to fund a meth habit (I pray, therefore, that this lessens their culpability). Nevertheless, Dawkins had seen on television a documentary about indulgences and such and must have come to believe in the wealth of every man of the church the world over. Once the body was dug up, they were hoping to find a skeleton emblazoned with jewels and precious metals. What they discovered was something much more startling but much less scandalous.

The odor of the body was not horrific but rather sweet. This was a shock, one that Cobb believed to be the sign of a kind of curse. Dawkins brushed off the notion and squashed his hesitancy. Like coroners, they examined the body with small flashlights, beginning with the tips of the fingers. All that was discovered was a simple ring and a metal cross that had fallen into the ribcage, items of little worth in the eyes of a covetous world.

It was when the light shined upon the skull for more than a moment that a discovery of inestimable beauty and value was revealed. Inside the jaw of this fallen priest lay an incorrupt tongue, pink and fleshy, glimmering with saliva as if the man had continued speaking while the rest of him rotted away. Cobb screamed and backed away like a man who had seen a ghost.

"Cursed! It's cursed!" he said before tripping over a tombstone.

Dawkins approached and struck him in the gut. "Shut up, you idiot! Do you have any idea what this is worth, what this can fetch us? This will be the last corpse we ever dig up."

"I don't care; put it back. Close it up!"

"Every body part, every jewel, every ring rolling around in the trunk added together will not even touch the money that we'll get for this one. So shut it!"

Cobb was, once again and without warning, overwhelmed by a proximate passion for drugs. He shook off his fears and pointed the light like a gun at the threatening jaw, to which the living tongue was still attached. The skull was ripped from the spine with the aid of a large knife and thrust into a brown duffle bag. It was tied up with an old shoelace. Cobb was handed this sack as well as the knife. Like a mother cradling a child, he secured the head in his lap as the pair drove from the cemetery in the direction of town.

The torment within that man must have been unbearable. Clearly, as was evidenced by my discovery in the confessional, his conscience, like burning iron rods, scalded him from the inside, cauterizing his heart, scarring it as a shield from the evil of the present moment. On the other hand, the dopamine and anticipated rush of a hit of meth rolled over in his mind like a refreshing wave, and drops of the cool water rippled through his veins. He bruised his skull on the window by repetitious banging. I anticipate that, when that automobile is discovered with or without Dawkins, the passenger window will be, if not cracked, stained with the same blood as my church floor.

They stopped for gas two blocks from this church, as the police report indicates. Dawkins went inside. Cobb sobbed and ground his teeth like corn at the miller. His eyes spun within their sockets, and he untied the sack. He drew out the skull with a grip so tense that the jaw broke. He removed his coat and rolled the head of Father Doyle up in it. A few skulls were stored in the trunk, a sort of malicious rolling mausoleum, and Cobb dropped one into the sack.

But what of the tongue? When Dawkins peered in and observed it missing, then Cobb's motives would be discovered. He'd be a dead man. Without hesitation of any kind, I believe Cobb used the knife from the graveyard to cut out his own tongue. How could a man of sane mind do such a thing as that? This is precisely the point: he was not of sane mind. His heightened conscience and nerves dulled by a cold and imaginary dopamine gave him no time to consider consequences of any sort. This was a thoughtless act, for after placing it inside the new skull, the blood began to overflow from his mouth. His only choice was to abandon the car and traverse the road in search of help.

Dawkins returned to the vehicle. "Where are you going? Get back here!" he yelled. "I swear to God if you…"

Cobb ignored him and spit a trail of blood along the sidewalk. Consciousness was fading. Dawkins split. Cobb entered through the doors of Saint Patrick's, found the stack of cards, scribbled his story, abandoned his coat, and returned to the threshold where he lay until discovered by Mrs. Juniper.

Your Excellency, before I turn this coat over to the police, I decided to write you in order to request that you be the fourth to see its contents. Please come immediately.

I began this letter by stating that my purposes were twofold. As you can see, not only did Dawkins not assault Cobb and cut out his tongue, but he also is not in possession of the head of Father John Doyle. It is now obvious to me that the word that Cobb desperately desired that I decipher on the marble steps of my parish was not "Confession," but rather, "Confessional." I still however, hold out hope for the forgiveness of his sins and have scheduled a visit to him tomorrow morning.

And now to address my original intention and more urgent purpose in drafting this letter. As pastor of Saint Patrick Catholic Parish and successor of the deceased, I hereby request, given the evidence of his holy stance before the Lord our God and the miraculous fingerprint left by Him, that Your Excellency immediately petition to the Holy See so as to initiate a Cause for the Beatification and Canonization of Father John Doyle, Requiescat in Pace.

In Christ,
Father Dominic Parker
Saint Patrick Catholic Parish

Invasive Species

It was July, the rainy season. Mikaela had hired Aarav, an Indian guide who spoke both English and Hindi in addition to several more localized languages. The rainy season rendered Mikaela uncomfortable and insecure. She was tall and thin, a pole of a woman, her craggy nose an icon of the rest of her. The turquoise raincoat about her body hung like a towel draped across the back of a navy chair. Only her eyes were horizontal, and they raked across her field of vision. She sniffled at a troupe of boys throwing rocks at one another along the road.

From the back seat, Savannah, pinched in by her navy blouse, was more like Mikaela's warm shadow with those dark eyebrows and cartoon eyes. Mikaela, she thought, was the obvious choice: the will, the medical training, and the determination to let her 'yes' mean 'must.' Had Savannah volunteered for this? That is a complicated matter, but the organization insisted she, being kind of dark-skinned and having studied abroad, fit the mold of a missionary better than they. The moral imperative, that is, the unmet need and the diminishing quality of life, was less an objective than a field of wonder. The longing for her husband, the strength of his charisma, was the thought wrapped up in her nausea. Her light brown legs were stuck to the cracked, mustard leather of the rattletrap sedan. The image of her husband sloshed across her mind, but she swallowed the thought as the road flattened and stretched as if awakening.

They abandoned the car in the little Indian village, which was overrun with monkeys, second-class citizens of a begging, thieving type of bother. At the café, Aarav placed before the two of them a plate of rice and vegetables. Across a small hill at the end of the road, the edge of the forest awaited them, an ominous milestone, more like a cave than the Connecticut forests they were accustomed to. Its screeching howls reached out, a far-off haunting, and penetrated with their flesh-like claws. For a moment, Savannah was lost in it as if hypnotized. Aarav stared with suspicion at the black backpacks, six in total, which encircled the trio.

"What medicine is it? What kind?" Aarav wondered aloud. "You have said it is medicine. I believe this. What kind? Many of my people suffer."

Mikaela sniffed. "The kind that all people need, the stuff of human rights."

"Vitamin? Antibiotic?"

Savannah, who could not bring herself to eat a single bite of food, jumped into the conversation. "Aarav, how many brothers do you have? How many sisters?"

The guide smiled, revealing his teeth to have a surprising dazzle. "Ah, six brothers, three sisters! Some are not with us any longer." Each word was a struggle, like it had to be pulled from his lungs. "I do miss them and my mother."

"Imagine," pushed Mikaela, "how your mother may have fared if—"

"Fared? What is the meaning of—"

Mikaela straightened and rephrased. "If your mother had had fewer, less children, it would have been easier for her? Yes? Would life have been simpler? Less to do for her? Less struggle?"

Aarav's face flattened as if struck with a mallet. "Yes, simpler," he seemed to get it. "However, I am the most small."

The Westerners did not understand. Savannah held up her hands to gauge his height compared to an invisible visitor. "Most small?"

"Oh, no," Aarav smiled. "No, I am most small, less age, least in age."

"The youngest?"

"Yes, youngest."

"Sometimes I wish that I had…" said Savannah with a solemnity, almost an adoration, in the direction of Aarav, but before she could finish, Mikaela's eyes devoured her own. "Um, sometimes I wish I had more experience with this kind of thing."

The odd trio finished the food in silence, which Mikaela broke only with her cavernous, dry sniffling. Savannah sipped her water drop by drop with micro-attention to make it, and the meal, span as much time as possible. Aarav looked into the long sky and signaled by a simple nod of his head that it was time.

The hike was not long, he assured them. A couple of kilometers through the jungle. There was a path. The tribe would be waiting on them. The women were handed machetes. "I clear," said Aarav, "but we all kill."

"Kill what?" the girls said together.

"Snakes." Aarav held up his arm like a puppet. "Cobras. You know this, then. Cobras?"

The girls nodded.

They saw no snakes. To be sure, there were plenty about them, but the crashing waves of tall grass enveloped them like heavy blankets. The screeching of the insects were syringes to their eardrums; there was no use trying to talk. Most often, Savannah walked backwards in the rear with a firm grip on the machete. Her other hand cradled her mouth, holding in the nausea. She envied Mikaela's confidence and tried to shake off the image of human skulls upon sticks warning trespassers to proceed with caution or not at all. If a passerby had seen them traversing the forest, they might have thought Mikaela, towering above the others, to be some kind of queen or goddess, carried by her subjects upon a sedan chair.

They entered a clearing as if passing through a threshold. It was all very sudden. A few women recognized Aarav and greeted him as if a hero; he had done this before. Suspicious, yet hopeful, glances were cast at the two Americans. Savannah and Mikaela exchanged looks. Savannah found the burgundy garb of the women to be both simple and beautiful, as if they were clothed with themselves. One of the women adorned Savannah with a crimson sash that devoured the navy blue of her blouse with a kiss. Mikaela refused it. With a cavernous smile, Aarav returned to them.

"I told them you bring medicine, come with medicine. I told them that you are a doctor. They are bringing the sick."

Mikaela grabbed his shoulder and spoke through gritted teeth. "Okay, I will see a few sick, but that's not why we're here. Tell them we have a different type of medicine for them. Ask for a group of women to gather later, like in an hour."

Aarav did as she requested. Savannah lined up the backpacks and stood at Mikaela's side as the doctor examined a few sick persons. To those to whom Mikaela could deliver good news, she did so; to those to whom she could not, she gave vague answers. Yes, that tooth should be pulled. No, without an MRI, there was no way to tell. Put it in a splint and rest. Sorry, no antibiotics.

When the line dwindled that afternoon, the women of the village were assembled in the clearing. Children dashed about them like rabbits through the brush. One man, wrapped in a fiery maroon fabric, seated himself in the center of the women as if they were all his daughters. This was the chief. Aarav said he had requested to be present.

Mikaela and Savannah zipped open the backpacks and passed the pills about until each woman possessed multiple cartridges, a supply of two years for each woman. The visitors began their presentation, which they had rehearsed for months. When to take the pills, how to do so, their effects, the risks of missing a morning. All of this Aarav translated. Faces hardened. Did Aarav tell them more; did he expand upon their message? Enthusiasm, necessity, duty: these are difficult to translate. Images of Indian-American families with one or two children were pulled from a backpack and passed among the gazes of suspicious eyes.

During Savannah's passionate statistical analysis, interrupted every so often by a dizzy spell, many of the women dropped the pills to the ground. Some were spit on, others were ground into the dirt with the heels of dirty feet. The women whispered. Mikaela wore a hardened look; Savannah knew its meaning. How did they not get it, not understand? Did they not know the simplicity of what was being handed on to them? Simpletons, pre-suffrage women under the thumb of stronger men. The pair would go to Africa next time. All the while, the chief, this man, sitting upright like a gargoyle, an icon of the past, gripped his staff like judge or jury or god or all of the above.

As if to do battle with their secret thoughts, the chief stood with mechanistic precision. The hush over the audience carried across them and into the souls of the trio of presenters. His stick was thrust into the ground, and he shouted one word repeatedly.

Aarav leaned in; "He says, 'Enough!'"

The chief changed tone. His face softened, his posture clicked. His smile showed his yellow teeth and, between them, he shouted something to the crowd, whose whispers rose to grunts and conversation and even laughter. Even many of the little children, not understanding, lit up like so many small stars. Before Aarav could explain, the chief approached Mikaela and Savannah and kissed their fingers before falling to one knee.

"He wants to ask you a question," said Aarav to Mikaela.

With the look of a long-lost lover, the chief swiveled his eyes back and forth between the pair before whispering something in the local language. In Savannah's mind, it was perhaps the most hopeful sentence ever muttered by human lips, as if trees could talk or wind whisper. Their presentation had worked; stats do not lie.

"The chief wants to know," Aarav muttered from the bottom of his throat. "He wants to know if it will work on snakes."

The girls paused. Mikaela lifted her sniveling head like a crane, an overarching figure, a titan of truth, a missionary, a holier-than-thou. "Excuse me, but snakes?" she questioned back.

Aarav translated. "Yes, snakes. Two of their children have died in the last year from cobra bites. Will the pills work on snakes?"

Mikaela opened her mouth to say no but was undercut by Savannah, who had fallen into the deep pools of the wise eyes of the chief. "Perhaps," she said unknowingly. "There's a chance it may work on snakes too."

The chief turned and yelled an exclamation to the women, all of whom gripped the pills in both hands and scooped them out of the dirt and carried them back to their huts and husbands. Aarav escorted the women to a gazebo-like structure for a rapid dinner; they had to be out before sunset, he said.

As Mikaela's jaw rose and fell upon the small bit of rice and meat that had been laid before her, Savannah watched a spectacle unfold of which they had been the catalysts. Men of the village shoved the pills into the ears and down the throats of baby monkeys, which let out howls rivaling the sirens of a crime scene. A number of rats or mice were victims of this baiting as well. The men were sent out by the chief, who laid his hands upon their shoulders and butted foreheads with each of them. Areas known to be heavy in snake activity were descended upon and baited so as to feed these small mammals to hungry cobra mothers guarding their eggs.

It was time to leave.

Mikaela was first to go and hacked at the underbrush as if bored. Savannah followed Aarav to the edge of the otherworldly jungle. She let him go ahead and turned her head for one last look at the people she would never see again. The chief stood as resolute as truth with what must have been his grandchildren circling him like planets around a sun. Savannah lifted her left hand and waved, and as the light refracted about the diamonds in her engagement ring, she placed her free hand on her womb. It was her needs that had been met, and she stepped into the mystery of the forest a freer woman.

Talitha Koum

When new meets old, the old loses. Even if what is old is true, it will bow at the altar of New, at least eventually. This is what made the neighbor, Mrs. Donna Periwinkle, the worst kind of person. She embraced the children of the New as if they were her own. Martha's husband Sam had always spoken of progress, but progress into what? Where you're progressing from and what you're progressing into must surely be more important than the progressing itself. Sam would say to put the wind at your back and see where it takes you.

The bathroom in which she was standing smelled like bleach, which she had sprayed across the moldy tile in the shower. Martha widened her eyes and blinked heavily to get a good look through the blotchy bathroom window. George Periwinkle's car rolled into the driveway that held hands with her property line.

She unlatched the window, which shrieked like a witch as it was ripped open. "Mr. Periwinkle, Mr. Periwinkle!"

"Good afternoon, Mrs…" He paused. "Ms. Setters, what may I do you for? My tires did not encroach on your property again, did they?"

"No, I do not believe they did, but you should know that your wife is wasting your money away like the sun wastes the ice."

Upon hearing the word "money," which he had plenty of, he became interested. "How so?"

"Every day, the children up and down the street come to her door after school lets out for candy and chocolate and..." What else was there?

"Cookies too."

"Yes, sir, those are the ones! Every day, those vagabonds wander to your door and feed off of her like babies at the breast!"

"Ms. Setters, my wife loves the children; I certainly can't help that! She says it's for happiness and the common good and the—"

"The only good, common or otherwise, from this situation is that the local dentists are making a pretty penny on all the teeth holes your wife is digging with her handouts. High demand, high prices, which explains the atrocious dental insurance rates." Ms. Setters had little idea as to the cost of a teeth cleaning, let alone the dental insurance rates.

Mr. Periwinkle loosened his tie, a move that Martha thought to be quite rude. "Ms. Setters, I will discuss your concerns with my wife, who I am sure will take them, for your sake, to heart."

"Her heart is too full; tell her to take them to her head!" Martha slammed the window, which cracked the glass. She lifted it once more and added, "And tell her that bridge will begin on time this week. We don't have time for her hair to set!"

Before his death, Sam had revealed to Martha exactly how much money he had left her, how often it would be filtered into her account, exactly how he had financially provided for her after his death in every way imaginable, and how if she ever followed through on her threat to vote Democrat, he would roll over in his grave. Mr. Setters' lawyer, Chase McCollum, revealed these same details a second time after his death. Even after the government confiscated its percentage, it was enough for Martha to retire on. Thank God.

She hadn't worked a day outside the home since the fall of the Berlin Wall when she was 34. That was a stake into the heart of social balance. Instability, like vulnerability, was an evil greater than death. No one gathered children for cookies in East Germany. However, there was nothing that could keep out these invasive families after Drake Automotive announced the construction of the new plant outside of the small town. This neighborhood was once entirely the property of her farming parents. She and Sam had sold most of it off when they were young and broke and stupid like most of these new people.

There was a knock at the door. Martha grunted and opened it. "Is it Wednesday already, Patrick?"

This lanky kid was only sixteen. His family moved here for his father, who worked at a supply plant that the paper was calling the town's savior. Their home directly across the street was a white cottage plucked from the pages of a magazine. "And take off that awful cap in the presence of a lady."

"Yeah…"   He ran his fingers through his hair. "…it's Wednesday." His thumbs tapped like a spider's legs on the screen of his cell phone.

"Yes, ma'am, to you, young man!" She almost hit him.

"Yes, ma'am; it is Wednesday." He put his phone in his pocket.

"And your parents know that you are here?"

"Yeah, um, yes, ma'am."

Martha began to shuffle through her wallet. A button fell out. Patrick picked it up. "When you get home, tell your parents that your younger siblings could use a few of those microchips they put in dogs to make sure they don't get lost." Dr. Bernard, the veterinarian, was the source of this technological information. He had been in business in Douglas for as long as she could remember. His official charge for service was always a fixed dollar amount, "Or, just, whatever ya' got." His children were some of the last of the Well-Behaved and left home for Mobile or Auburn or both years ago. "I swear to the Good Lord," Martha finished, "I saw your sister walking down the middle of Highway 84 just yesterday."

Patrick sighed. "Yes, ma'am."

She began to count out the dollar bills. "Has your father lost his job to a robot yet? You know it's only a matter of time."

"No, ma'am; do you need the same things today?" He held out the list she had sent with him a week ago.

"Read it to me again."

"Milk, eggs, two rotisserie chickens, rice, butter, broccoli, a bag of frozen peas, coffee, half and half, strawberries, blueberries, any other good-looking fruits, Sister Shubert's, and powdered donuts."

"Yes." Martha spit the word out as if a bug had flown into her mouth. "Double the donuts, no peas, and only get the berries if they're from Florida. Nothin' from Brazil. Something in the soil down there makes 'em sour. Oh, and cornbread mix." She handed him sixty dollars and told him to keep the change, as usual.

"I'm sorry, ma'am. I doubt that'll be enough today," Patrick said.

"What's that? You selfish child!"

"Ms. Setters, you haven't heard about the chicken shortage?" Patrick checked his legs for mosquitoes.

"What on God's green earth are you talkin' about? There ain't no chicken shortage. Alabama practically raises as many chickens as the rest of the world combined." This fact Martha had gathered from Veronica Griggs, a member of her bridge group. She was wisdom personified and always backed up her conclusions with the facts.

"Some disease killed about a hundred thousand or more of them or something like that. They cost double right now. I asked my mom before I came over here just to make sure."

Martha shook her finger at him. "If you're makin' this up, Patrick Spade, I swear I'll find someone else to waste my money on; y'understand?" She handed him another twenty dollars.

"Yes, ma'am," Patrick replied with what looked like a smirk. They both knew that there was no chicken shortage, and Martha had no way of finding out without making a fool of herself. Even though it pained Martha to send a representative of herself out in public in a cotton t-shirt, he was the only child within a stone's throw with a driver's license. He was irreplaceable. Two years ago, the doctor ordered her to stop driving after she ran off the road and into a light post. Martha's argument that there were fewer light posts when she was growing up was unconvincing.

As Patrick turned to leave, another man, well-groomed and well-dressed, waited at the bottom of the stairs that led to the porch. He cleaned his glasses with a small cloth and cleared his throat more than once. In his hand, he held a small gift with cheap red wrapping and secured with a white paper ribbon. The former gave it away as dispensable and of no value. The value of a gift is in the eye of the beholder. Veronica Griggs said as much.

Before she turned her attention to him, Martha saw, out of the corner of her eye, a small girl of eight or nine leaning against the banister of the porch next door. She was watching. Martha turned to her. "We don't need an audience!" The little girl scrambled inside.

"Ms. Setters," said the man as he climbed the stairs. "I beg your pardon, ma'am. I am Jackson Caldwell, president of the neighborhood association. May I have a quick word? It is a pleasure to finally speak to you in person."

"You say 'finally' as if I were avoiding you. Am I a cancer to which you have 'finally' succumbed?"

He blushed. "No, ma'am, of course not. It's just that, well, ma'am, you are a difficult person to reach. You must be very busy."

She knew what he meant. Martha had unplugged her phone from the wall during a lightning storm and never plugged it back in. Not only that, but out of principle, she refused to answer the door between Friday and Sunday. "I am extremely busy, yes. What do you want, sir, and what is a neighborhood association?"

After he explained the concept, Martha told him that there was no such thing before Drake Automotive built the plant. She had lived here long before there was a neighborhood the size of a small town encroaching upon her sense of privacy, and for this reason, she wasn't paying a dime to support any such thing.

"As a resident of the neighborhood, ma'am, even if you refuse to pay the dues, you are still subject to the bylaws."

"Oh, get to the point, Mr. Caldwell. As we have mutually agreed, I am very busy."

"Your property needs beautification."

"Speak English."

"You need to cut your grass."

Martha asked him if he thought that her old bones could push a lawnmower. He said of course not but that the late Mr. Setters always hired one of the children from the neighborhood to cut it. He fiddled with his glasses again. Martha replied that, as a widow, she hadn't the money but that she did have a lawyer who knew the law of Alabama better than Atticus Finch. Mr. Caldwell seemed ignorant of what this meant.

"In short," Martha said firmly and with finality, "God made the grass to grow, but if you want it shorter, then you are welcome to come and cut it yourself."

"Yes, ma'am," Mr. Caldwell said. "I will have it taken care of." He bowed his head and walked north up Carnet Court. At the end of the cul-de-sac, he entered the new construction with a blue door.

The little girl next door was lying down on the porch and watching between the rails of the banister. Martha gave her a look, shut the door and opened the present. On a keychain was a piece of metal engraved with the words "Burrough Heights" in cursive. A flower bloomed beneath the 'B.'

The widow sat down to write a note: "I am in no need of a keychain, Mr. Caldwell. A person my age is likely not in need of it because they have lost the keys to put upon it. When they have found these same keys, they still are not in need of a keychain.

If you have a child approaching the driving age, then I suggest you save it for him or her. Please accept it in return for lawn service." When Patrick returned, she gave him a nickel to walk the present and note to the Caldwell's mailbox. He didn't argue.

It was true that the home had fallen into disrepair, a process that began with Mr. Setters' diagnosis seven years ago. His slow and steady decline did not fail to catch the attention of the papers. Stories of Sam Setters, his failures and successes in politics and public life, fueled the paper like gasoline for an engine or like facts for Veronica. Little else in the small town could make the front page, really any page for that matter. There was not a position that he had failed to run for in the state of Alabama, including governor (which he lost in a landslide) and city council (which he won hands down). He died a state senator. This lifestyle was a burden to Martha, and she could not bring herself to subject children to the same level of scrutiny she had suffered. She did not want little Setters children who could become the worst kind of people. Her husband did not protest this decision, like many of hers, at least not out loud.

Christopher the cat did not protest either. He was once a beautiful calico but had grayed in equal measure with Martha over the last few years. She was not sure how, but Christopher came and went in and out of the home as he pleased. Martha had opened the door for him in the last few months as often as she had paid for his vet bills. This was not at all. Dr. Bernard shook his head at her wallet and always said that Sam Setters had done enough for him and this town, whatever that meant. Nevertheless, one minute Christopher was rubbing against her legs and the next was crouched in the high grass as if he were young enough to catch a squirrel.

This in and out did not bother Martha. Her parents had once left town for a funeral and had to search for three days to find the house key so as to lock the door. In those days, you were safe. It was assumed. If you were not home for supper, you were at the Dorton's or the Frank's, and you would be home by 7:30.

There was another knock at the door. Martha unhitched the lock and flung it open. It was Markus Tindale, Pastor of the Three Peaks Methodist Church. The church of Martha's upbringing, United Methodist, underwent rebranding under the leadership of this young man. Martha could not bring herself to attend the church run by a man with tattoos on his arms and who knows where else. His mother, though, was excellent at bridge and concluded that the good that came from his entering the seminary canceled out the evil of the tattoos.

"Markus, how may I be of service to you?"

He wore long sleeves at all times, the formality of which was only a side effect of their true purpose. "Please, call me Pastor Mark," he said as he leaned on a wooden cane.

Martha had remembered the car accident. "Pastor Mark, how can you even begin to climb the Three Peaks with a bad leg?"

"By the grace of God, ma'am." At least he had manners. "I came to check on you, Ms. Setters. Is there anything that I can do for you?"

Martha knew this question to be sincere. "No."

He chuckled. "I have not seen you in church in quite a while, Ms. Setters. My mother says that you say that you've been going to church in your heart. This may be true—I wouldn't begin to deny it—but I need not remind you of the Fourth Commandment in light of Christ's command to-"

"No, you need not remind me. Besides, we got enough Jesus in the South to go around."

"You can never have enough Jesus, ma'am."

"If Jesus were to ride the New York subway, they wouldn't even sit next to him, wouldn't even acknowledge him."

"We may sit next to Jesus down here or throw an arm around his shoulders like we're good pals, but we are still just as hesitant as anyone to bend the knee."

Martha gave the stare she put on when she knew she had been outdueled. It bought her time. Before she could open her mouth, he asked the question.

"What time may I pick you up this Sunday? Service begins at 8:30."

She gave a sigh as quick as the wind and said 8:00 before shutting the door.

✠

When he picked her up that Sunday, she remarked on the traffic that comes with overpopulation. This theory was cemented when she saw the new Catholic Church, built to accommodate the new families from the north. Markus said there could never be too many people any more than there could be too many flowers. Martha reminded him that some flowers are weeds.

Church that Sunday went rather regular (she was probably saved but could not remember exactly). Except for the eyes. Eyes were on her. Everywhere, eyes. Even the eyes of children. She wanted to stand up and shout, "Yes, I am the wife of the late Sam Setters. Yes, he acted like an idiot out in public and said some crazy things and made good and bad decisions like everyone else, but he's dead now, so get over it." But she didn't. The eyes were worse when a church announcement was cut short. It began, "This Tuesday there will be another meeting to, um…" and the lector shuffled through her papers as if a bug crawled across them after awkwardly catching her eyes. What was the ending of the announcement? Did it have to do with her? She lifted her chin up high, but the lector stepped away from the podium.

When Markus ("Pastor Mark, please, ma'am") dropped her off at home, she entered to find a peculiarity. On her kitchen table was a rose, freshly cut. She examined it. Whoever had cut it did so perpendicular to the stem. She thought of old boyfriends who could have returned but shut them out.

A hidden voice came to her from another room like a phantom. "Do you like it?"

Martha turned quickly and would have grabbed a knife if the tone were not so innocent. There in the hallway was the little girl from next door. She was beautiful, as beautiful as the rose. Her smocked dress was typical for a Lower Alabama Sunday. Martha's heart began to stir, but she shut it down, permitting it instead to beat like a snare drum.

"My goodness, child, how did you get in here?"

The girl began to walk around the living room, looking at the pictures in the frames. "Do you like it?"

"Why, child, I..." Martha paused. This girl's father was one of the new ones, probably a Catholic and certainly a contributor to the overpopulation.

"No, I am..." Martha searched for an excuse. "I am allergic. Take it away, child, take it away! My fingers are too delicate for the thorns anyway." She returned the rose. Before she could tell her to never come back, the girl exited out the front door as if she had been invited in to begin with.

Martha vigorously searched for the cat's way in and way out. There was a hole in the siding that led to the crawlspace in the backyard. How a cat or person could enter the home crawling through this portal was beyond her. Nevertheless, she patched it with duct tape as if it were a bleeding wound.

Then it occurred to her. Had this girl stolen anything? She searched the home. Most everything appeared to be in order but for the door to an upstairs closet left ajar. She opened it fully and entered into the darkness. Old clothes hung around. Etched on the frame were the heights of she and her siblings as they grew up. The tail of an old kite on the upper shelf swung like the pendulum of a grandfather clock.

A few days passed as normal, but if it was not clear from Patrick's smirk the other day that the story of the chicken shortage was a scam, then the onslaught of young people requesting odd jobs gave it away. It was certainly the summer of solicitation. Twin boys asked to paint. A teenage girl asked if she had any grandchildren who needed babysitting and another if she could wash her windows. One brat had the nerve to ask if she needed help walking to the mailbox.

Thursday afternoon, Martha stood on the sidewalk and waited for Mrs. Periwinkle, who was characteristically sixty seconds late out the door just as she was late in bidding during bridge. As they walked, they bickered about the state of things and finally reached the threshold of

Veronica's home. This evening, their hostess admitted to hearing nothing about a chicken shortage and wondered why Martha asked. No reason, just a vicious rumor designed to hurt the economy. When Martha questioned Veronica about the new tablecloths on the counter, the subject was changed.

The evening ended without any drama, quite unusual, and Martha returned with Mrs. Periwinkle the way they had come. When Martha entered her front door, the little girl was standing in her living room, examining the photographs once more. The widow not only felt threatened but also intrigued by this girl's curiosity. The child spun and began to question her about what she observed in the frames.

"Was this your husband? What are you doing in this picture that has you laughing so much? Is that paint on your nose? Why don't you have any children, or do you? If not, it's funny how you're holding your stomach in this picture like my mom did when she was pregnant with my brother. Are these your parents? What is your daddy eating in this picture? My mommy puts up lots of pictures of our dogs, why don't you have any pictures of your cat?"

Martha eschewed these questions. "I have a better question for you, young lady. Why are you in my home?"

"I thought you might need someone to talk to."

"I have the Good Lord to talk to and my bridge club. Surely, you know that about me if you've the nerve enough to break into my home."

The little girl said nothing but pointed to the kitchen table. Her favorite dessert, one dozen brownies from Pulley's Bakery, awaited her.

"No, child, I'm sorry." Martha sent them the way of the rose. "These do not sit well with my stomach in my old age."

The girl strolled out the front door. Martha's eyes followed the brownies. Today's children were bolder and ruder, to boot. Quickly, Martha went out the back door to the hole in the crawl space. The duct tape was still there. She walked around, thinking of where this child could have entered. Her head spun. All but one window upstairs was locked, which she bolted and secured with duct tape for good measure.

✠

The following morning, an unfamiliar teen was mowing her lawn. With difficulty, he cut the thick grass that grew around the rusty light post that had adorned this property since she was a child. The weatherman on the radio had told her that the temperature was 93 degrees, but it felt like 103 with the humidity. If the child was smart, he would have brought with him a bottle of water. However, he was not smart. There was a knock at Martha's door. The child requested a glass of water, if it was not too much trouble. She could tell that he was not from around here, but she retrieved a glass for him nevertheless. A dead child on the lawn would have been too much trouble.

"Why don't you have any flowers? Hydrangeas grow very well around here." This child's question was extremely forthcoming and to the point, like that of a lawyer to a witness.

"Who told you to ask me that, child? Did Mrs. Periwinkle put you up to this, you little brat? I don't care about flowers in my yard any more than I care about unsolicited questions!"

The child's face told Martha that he regretted asking it. "No, I'm sorry. My mom, she said, um...never mind; thanks for the water." He handed the glass back to her after only one small sip and finished the lawn as if he were needed elsewhere.

This neighborhood, this community, these people, they were all against her. She was against them. She was a wart on the hand of progress, a stain on a new blouse, a storm in a new spring. She stood at the threshold staring into the windows of the surrounding houses. Stainless steel appliances in the kitchens. Flat-screen televisions broadcast football games in high definition. Children played video games and stared into their phones in the middle of the day as if the rays of the sun were a threat.

This was the New. It was terrifying. She was alone. Did someone just close the blinds on her across the street? The door creaked to a close. She looked out the window. The postman cast her a glance. Martha cried. Those who forget history are doomed to repeat it. She shut the history out of her mind. She was never married. This town was never her own. Where these houses stood was never her parents' farm. It was futile. The present was the new past. She threw a blanket over herself.

"Are you okay?" The little girl stood in the hallway.

Martha now hated this child. She was the New. Not even the walls of her house could keep It out. Like the artist who hates a rival, she hated the beauty of this child. Martha wanted to lash out at her, to spray her with the bottle of bleach. But she couldn't. Her muscles were too old. Her bones were too rusty. She could not move fast like she used to. "Go away!"

The child walked closer. She was holding a box in her hands that rattled with each step. "Will you play with me?" Within moments, she was sitting in an armchair. The box was set on the coffee table.

Martha turned around. The box was a game, Checkers. "Where did you get that?" She had not seen the box in years.

"At the top of a closet upstairs. Will you play with me?"

Martha smirked and sat up. She wiped her eyes with the blanket and threw it off. Who was this curious child? She reached her hand for the box but thrust it back. Martha stood up and busied herself around the living room.

"No, child, I am sorry," she said. "I am far too busy, and my arthritis will not allow me to play without severe pain. Go put that game back where you got it."

The girl obeyed. When she returned, she stood once more staring at the pictures. "Your wedding anniversary is next Wednesday. Do you have any plans to celebrate?"

Martha paused, shocked. She finished dusting a small crystal angel and placed it back on the shelf as if this question did not rattle her. "How did you know that—"

"Were you really born in this house?"

"Why, child, I... how did you... I don't know where you got your information from."

The little girl stared at the pictures and pointed to a matching set of three frames. In the first, a woman in a wedding dress. In the second, a man carrying that same woman across a threshold. In the third, the same man and woman, smiling joyfully, painting the light post in the front yard a beautiful white.

"Is this you?" the little girl asked.

"That was me, but things have changed."

"Is this your husband?"

"That was him, yes."

"Is the house in these pictures the same as the one you're living in now?"

"Yes."

"The one you were born in?"

Martha stared into the little girl. "Yes."

"Are you pregnant in this picture?"

Martha didn't answer but began to cry once more. She had never told her husband about the miscarriage.

The girl exited the front door. Martha did not know if she hated this child or loved her as her own. Was she even real? Were hallucinations common at her age? She ran to the mirror in the bathroom and stared, not at herself, but the reflected scene around her in search of more mirages. Martha leaned forward and examined her pupils like a doctor, expecting the image of the beautiful girl to be etched into them. She wasn't there. Martha went to sleep.

✠

The child was right; next Wednesday was her anniversary. When the day came, Martha waited as usual an extra minute or so for Mrs. Periwinkle to trump down the steps. They could not walk today. Mrs. Tindale was the hostess and lived outside of the city limits. Mrs. Periwinkle drove, and terribly slowly.

In the car, Martha opened her mouth to speak, but shut it. Finally she mustered the courage. "Do you know the little girl next door to me?"

"Yes." Her answer was uncharacteristically short.

"So, she exists." Martha paused. "I mean, she really lives there."

"Yes."

"Donna, how can we do it?"

"Do what?"

"How can we survive all this? All this change?"

Donna got to the heart of things. "On a scale of one to ten, how lonely are you?"

"Oh, don't act like you know me! Did Veronica tell you to ask me that?"

"I can see it in your eyes, sister!"

These were the last words that were spoken before they rolled up the driveway of the Tindales. Where were the other cars?

On the door was a note. *We have the flu. Bridge canceled. Come back next week.*

"Hmph," Martha said. "A phone call would have been nice!"

Donna was sending a text message on her phone.

"You know how to do that!" Martha exclaimed.

Donna smiled and walked back to the car.

As they drove back, a metal sign spanned the width of the road at the corner of Carnet Court. "ROAD CLOSED FOR CONSTRUCTION."

"Well, Lord above!" Martha threw her hands in the air. "What in the world could they be building at this hour? Probably another neighborhood full of brats."

"Probably just some road work," Donna said. "We'll need to park on Ashville Road and use the cut through into my backyard."

They parked in front of one of the newer homes and trespassed through the yard and into the driveway of the Periwinkles. Martha rounded the corner of her home as she made her way to the front door. She stopped short and gasped.

Her front yard was flooded with people: Mr. Periwinkle, the mayor, Mrs. Tindale and her son, children everywhere, and it was certainly the first and last time that a priest would ever set foot on her property.

"Surprise!"

Martha didn't know what to say. The urge welled up in her to shout at them to get off her property. As she opened her mouth to shut them out, she noticed out of the corner of her eye the little girl from next door. She was walking toward Martha.

Martha bent down and placed her hand on her head to make sure she was real. "Child, I have spoken with you many times but have never asked your name."

"Bella," she said. The little girl held out her hand to shake Martha's but didn't let go. Instead, Bella led her to the light post. On the ground was a can of white paint and new paintbrushes. Martha glanced around once again and noticed various tools, plants, paint, and cleaning supplies. They waited for her to speak and took pictures with their phones. She resisted the urge to send them away.

The mayor held up a glass. "A toast," he said, "to Ms. Martha Setters and to the late Sam Setters!" He handed her a key to the city. The people placed gifts and notes on a table and started with their work both in and out of the home. Pastor Mark rolled up his sleeves, set to work with the priest. Martha scuttled across the lawn and read some of the notes. Many of them thanked her husband, whose policies and influence were responsible for bringing Drake Automotive to town in the first place. If he had told her that in life, she probably would have killed him before the cancer. Martha returned to the light post.

The can of paint was popped open, and a paintbrush was put into her hand. Martha turned to the girl. "How did you get into my home all this time? Who put you up to this?"

"Your husband gave me a key. He said I was the only person on the block you wouldn't hit with a pan. He asked if I'd try to bring you a few gifts and maybe play some games to draw you out before it came to this!"

"And the light post was his idea?"

"No, mine."

Martha took the brush and dipped it into the paint. The brush swept like a gentle snowfall over the metal that had been scraped of its rust. Upstairs in her home, the grime on the windows was being wiped away. Pure light, unfiltered, entered in through them and illuminated the new faces that had entered her home uninvited but now welcome.

Apathy

An army of youth, self-programmed for stability, stood in formation hemmed in by the four walls that they themselves had built. There was no need for a roof. Despite the biting chill of the breeze that blew the hair about their stoic faces, they remained lukewarm. The rain began to fall and stung their cheeks like acid. Apathy moved among them like a phantom, and every so often, she would stop and stare into the face of one of them. Despite her horror, not a soul was stirred.

She stopped and spun around like a bat in the night, pivoting on the old feet hidden beneath her rotting cloak. Somewhere, a shoulder had twitched. She raced among them like a snake through the tall grass and stared into the eyes of many. One of them blinked; it was a young man in a red button-down shirt. The witch lifted her yellow hand with long, curling fingernails and, like a viper, gripped his ear; with all her might, she yanked it towards the floor. Blood ran down the side of his face and was carried away by the rain. Like a slot machine, his brown eyes rolled over in his head until they snapped to a stop. His head fell forward. Apathy let out a low cackle through her sly smile.

"It is raining," she said to him, "and you have no umbrella."

"Who cares?" the youth asked in reply.

"You are bleeding," the witch remarked as if concerned.

"So what?" the young man said.

She breathed on him a putrid gas from her raspy lungs, and he fell even more still, as if in a trance, and stared into a small screen where his palm used to be. He was lost in it. Suddenly from the other side of the room, there was a sneeze. With a hiss, the witch raced about, splashing the legs of the young with each step. The trickle of the water spiraling down the drain in the center of the room echoed off of the walls and into the open sky. Apathy came to a stop. There she was, a young lady with blue eyes made darker by the dark hair that hugged her cheeks. Beneath her green and gold blouse, she was shivering. The witch moved close and, like a caring mother, put her hand to the smooth forehead. The young lady was cold. Apathy yanked at her ear without hesitation. The eyes rolled and rolled but snapped to a stop backwards. The girl was looking into herself.

"No!" gasped the witch, and again she checked her temperature, which was rising by the second.

"Why..." the girl said as her voice trailed off.

The witch screamed in her face and yanked at the other ear to fix the malfunction. The eyes spun and stopped, to the relief of Apathy, in the proper direction. Trails of blood dripped from her split ends.

Through browning teeth and only inches from her beautiful young face, the witch whispered to her, "You are bleeding."

"So what?" the girl replied.

"Do you know who you are, and why you have no umbrella?"

"Does it matter?" The blue eyes did not blink even once.

With a coy smile, the witch breathed on her, and the lovely head fell forward to stare into her palm. The witch doubled her efforts and glided from youth to unsuspecting youth, checking their foreheads and asking them questions. When Apathy reached the far corner, a sharp clap reverberated throughout the room. The witch reeled and saw out of formation the young girl who had malfunctioned and seen into herself. She had clapped her palms together, showering specks of shattered glass about her like glitter. The young girl ran to the drain and lifted the grate above her head as she stared into the rain.

"You cursed child!" yelled the witch.

The girl threw down the grate and the noise stirred more than a few of the others. She jumped into the sewers. As the sharp glass and warm blood from her splintered palms were carried to the feet of others by the water, those who had stirred began to lift their heads and mutter words in deep voices, and some who had not yet awoken began to twitch or shiver. Apathy scrambled about the room, breathing on whomever she could and lifting palms to faces. When she passed through the spot where the young girl in the green blouse had once stood, she gasped, for the air was quite warm.

Tohu wa Bohu

The priest with the chalky eyes snapped the wafer into Charlie's hand only after the boy said, "Amen." It had been a few tense seconds. The priest had bent low to offer him the Body of Christ, but Charlie leaned sideways like a curved pine to inspect the painting above the tabernacle. It caught his eye not only because it was new but also because he had seen it before, the hand of God with its index finger pointing and nearly touching the tip of another. Like a kindergartener's valentine, it stood for something beautiful but would not hold to the scrutiny of an art critic. "The Body of Christ," the priest said again with emphasis on the nouns.

Amen.

Whenever Charlie slipped the host into his mouth, he had the sense that it ought to be chewed differently, like licking and sealing an envelope without staining the paper or creasing the fold. His mother chewed dinner like that on days when she would kick off her shoes at the door and, like instinct, raise her outstretched arm to the top shelf where the wine glasses did not have the chance to gather much dust. The only other body that Charlie had bitten into was his sister's, which cost him a week of cartoons. He put up a fight. If he was that desperate to watch television, his father told him in the garage, then he could sit in his mother's lap and learn something about real life from the news because the secondhand school that the city was funneling him into next year would not be teaching him. If Claver Middle lived up to its reputation, then the only thing he'd be learning there was how to speak Spanish.

When his mother brought him and his sister to Mass, they sat in the back pew to the priest's right when he was facing the people. Charlie preferred these seats to his father's favorite row in the middle of the church because he heard the priest say once that God, in the end, consigned the good kinds of people and animals to his right and the bad to his left. Whenever churchgoers came in late out of the heat and through the side door, you could also be the first to look at them without their seeing you if your eyes were quick enough. Charlie had learned how to look at people from his mother. From what would be whispered to him throughout Mass, the boy often wondered why the priest did not mandate more of the sinners to sit at his left.

Minutes before falling in line with the march of communicants, as the altar bells chimed and Charlie shifted his weight from one knee to the next, his mother curled around the neck of his sister. She put her dry lips to his small ear.

"Six rows up, the man in the hideous gray suit. He's the councilman who voted to redraw the map."

Charlie studied the back of his head and tried to figure out how a man could redraw a map. Charlie pictured him as a much larger person with a bag of giant tools that could widen rivers and pull mountains from valleys. Whatever it was that the man could do, Charlie knew that it would cause him to go to a different school when August came. Something in him was excited about the change until he saw his mother's tears. This man hurt people with his maps.

Charlie let the wafer rest on his tongue as he walked step for step behind his mother, as close to her as he could without clipping her heels. They skipped the chalice. A brief flash of light shot into the church as the mapmaker exited through one of the double doors behind the altar. Like a whip, Charlie's mother grabbed his hand and yanked him through the side exit as his sister obediently followed. Almost like thieves, the three of them blazed a shortcut behind the shrubbery on the side of the church. Charlie's palm slipped from the grip of his mother, who, like a predator, rushed from the bushes and scurried into the parking lot, where she and the mapmaker began to argue.

His sister sat on the curb, and Charlie joined her, and he soon was dropping pebbles onto passing ants like some kind of god. The pitch and volume of the voices in the parking lot intensified, even as the two of them distanced themselves further from the church one small step at a time. His mother, clearly echoing pieces of the mapmaker's explanation, shouted big words like "population" and "rezoning." She was good at making people feel guilty. Beyond those two, through the mirage of the melting concrete, a small child that Charlie figured to be about his age hurled a tennis ball onto the roof of the church hall and tried catching it behind his back. After five tries, he finally achieved the feat and seated himself beneath the shade of a nearby oak.

Crowds began to pour through the doors like a pipe that had sprung a leak. Lines formed for coffee and donuts around two tables under the shade of an area for picking up and dropping off in the rain. Children ran in circles with sticky fingers, and grownups raised their voices to talk over one another as they cast quick glances at the exchange of words thirty yards distant. Families walked out of their way to avoid being in close proximity to the argument as they set out for their minivans and SUVs.

Charlie's mouth dried up. He needed fresh water, not orange juice, and as a fish swims upstream, he fought the crowds to reenter the church to sip from the water fountain at the back. What he found, instead, was the priest who, despite his failing knees, lay prostrate before the image. In the quiet, his deep whispers carried like a gentle breeze. The boy, so as not to interrupt, slowly backed out and rejoined his sister on the curb.

A few minutes past the close of Mass, a sizable crowd still lingered, and it polished off the remaining refreshments. Without warning, there was a loud crack and the breaking of glass. Everyone turned to gape at the man and woman nearly at each other's throats in the parking lot, and Charlie and his sister jumped to their feet. All were expecting to see one or the other of the quarrelers lying on the ground and bleeding, but instead, both Charlie's mother and the mapmaker were staring with looks of pure horror past the crowds and at the church doors. The noise, like an earthquake, roared a second time, and all pivoted to witness a giant fist with an index finger outstretched and breaking through the double doors. The hand was too wide for the square frame, which began to bulge and crack open like the breaking of a violent dawn. Shards of wood shot into the air, and the old bricks began to crumble like dry bread.

A mob of people, including the mother and the mapmaker, sprinted for the door. In this, they were all united. Both men and women bundled on either side of the extended index finger and shoved with all their strength. High heel shoes were flung off and sport coats thrown to the ground, and although a few men tried to grip a knuckle with their arms like pliers, the sweat of their hands made it nearly impossible to do so.

Fifteen seconds passed, then thirty, and neither party had advanced any further upon the other. Charlie could see the old priest through a window and made an oath that he would never tell his mother that the man of God was pushing the hand out with his cane and all the while whispering.

Like a fish pulled onto the dock, the hand began to shake side to side. The mob erupted like a volcano with a new surge of aggression, and some men jumped off the backs of others and onto the top of the hand. A couple of them were thrust onto the concrete sidewalk and more than a few took blows to the head from a falling piece of brick or mortar.

Charlie and his sister were the only two children who had not been corralled by three of the women behind a far-off automobile. A gust of wind surged forth from behind them and ripped napkins from under paper cups. A handful of dust and leaves were spun into a small whirlwind, which passed between Charlie and the fist and turned him towards it. He gasped. He was being drawn into the middle of the mayhem, and it was no longer his decision. A fisherman had hooked him, and he took a step in the direction of the church. His sister snatched the back of his belt for a moment but let it go, most likely thinking that Charlie was going to retrieve their mother. Despite the mob of adults, a path lay open before him to the hand since no one dared to go near the dangerous tip of the pointed finger. It beckoned him. In anticipation of his mother questioning his approach, Charlie tried to think up a reason to draw near to such an unbridled force, but none came to him. He was there, merely inches away, and in a strange embrace, he put one arm on top and one beneath in a hug of some kind and rested his head on the fingernail.

The finger withdrew itself from Charlie's grip and the multitude began to cheer. For a few brief seconds, it appeared as if they had succeeded in forcing the fist back into the church where it belonged. The men relaxed their grips, and those women who had been striking it with the heel of a shoe took a deep breath. Then, a flash of lightning. The finger struck Charlie in the chest with a viper's speed, and the boy was shot backwards like a rock from a slingshot. From the point of view of the gasping crowd, this was an assault that could not go without further beating, but to Charlie, it was the gentle kiss of his grandmother at the threshold of her home. Charlie's mother and a few other sweaty women converged on the boy lying prostrate on the asphalt.

The fist paused for a moment before sliding back into the hidden darkness of the church. The mapmaker and another man reached to close the doors, but upon seeing that they lay shattered on the ground and there was no frame to close them into, they stood guard until a pickup truck could be parked at the entrance as a barricade. Charlie was rolled over by the many hands, which then lifted his shirt and rubbed his rib cage to see if it was smashed to pieces. It was not, and Charlie rose to his feet.

The crowd took their time in departing the scene. Like a football team that has won a very close match, they stood around and panted with their hands on their heads. Some seemed eager to relay an eyewitness account to the police or a news camera. One man winced when he stepped on a shard of brick in search of his shoes but laughed it off, knowing that the worst was over. Others drifted from one person to the next, giving hugs and shaking hands, after all having found some common ground. Even Charlie's mother and the mapmaker momentarily embraced until, like ships with snapped anchors, they inevitably drifted once more into the rough waves of their worldly ideals, and the shouting match resumed.

Charlie did not share their relief. He wanted it back. It had met him, touched him, kissed him, befriended him. And then it left. Something was missing now, something that ought to be there. No, it was in him. On the tip of his tongue, at the front of his mind. Something. The finger had chosen him for a reason. He, apart from all the others, had beheld it behind the priest, who at this moment was weeping silently on the other side of a cracked window. He had been beckoned. Then it occurred to Charlie that the fist had not told him something but, rather, had asked him something.

The finger had planted in him a question, not an answer. There it was, springing up in his mind like the dawn, and in only a few moments, it sprouted and budded and bloomed. That is when Charlie, through a smile, gave his answer with the strength and peace of one whole breath: "Yes."

The boy turned on his heels and walked away.

"Where are you going?" his sister yelled to him.

"Come and see," he called back as he crossed the parking lot. The heat was more than heat out there. It was feeling; it was noise, and its hum was enough to frighten away many of the adults from following him, even if a part of them had wanted to. An ultimatum from his mother, commanding that he return, danced about him and remained with him as if it were an option. Charlie endured the sauna until he came to the shade of an oak tree, where the humming and the glare and the demands came to an end.

"Hey, what's your name?" Charlie asked the boy with the ball.

"Miguel."

"I'm Charlie. Where are you from?"

"My family just moved here a year ago," the boy said as he ground his feet into the dirt.

"Where do you go to school?"

"Claver Middle," Miguel responded.

"Hey, me too. Do you want to play wall ball? I used to play it at my old school all the time."

The boy blinked and turned his eyes away as a subtle smile flashed across his face like a ripple on a glassy sea. "Yes, but I do not know how."

"I'll teach you," Charlie said. "Let's play!"

The boy with the ball tossed it to Charlie, who flung it against the wall with enough speed to shatter a window. Charlie dropped the rebound and sprinted to the wall, laughing as if the other knew the rules. It was a teaching moment.

The Grand Prize

Two dozen children scurried to the glass countertop, a stampede. Sissy and her thin frame were felled to the hard carpet; her waves of dirty blond hair rippled across her plaid shoulders, hemmed in her long chin, and stretched for the glasses that had jumped from her face in the fall. Sissy reached out, but as her fingertips touched the rim of the frame, a wide, black sneaker crushed the left lens. She put them on and stood up again, anonymously blushing from embarrassment and envy twenty five feet from the edge of the small crowd. The glasses dripped off the end of her nose, which she wiped with her red-and-black sleeve.

The red, swirling lights and ear-piercing wail of the alarm drowned out the cacophony of colors and sounds from the games and machines about the arcade. Even the music from the dance pad, having been abandoned mid game, was neutered, but even so, not an ear would have noticed otherwise. Sissy sighed and sagged over a pinball machine. This was the Grand Prize; it had been won. More truly, it had been earned. Fifteen thousand tickets. The discipline, the saving, the bartering, the cost. Countless small choices, the risk of a jackpot, or slow and steady? Months or even years of calculation and a steadfast will were equally necessary for success.

Sissy stayed back and stood on the plastic seat of a race car to get some kind of view, made more difficult by her broken lens. It had been six months and eleven days since the alarm had been sounded, and before that, four months and eight days. The last time, it was a $300 gift card, and the time before, a brand new video game console.

Mr. Landry was the owner of the arcade, loved by all, respected by some, and feared by none. Even his raised voice was more like the echo of a real, far-off scolding. He was an ostrich of a man, carrying his weight at his hips, with a torso that thinned into his neck. To the cheers of dozens, he stepped on a small stool and reached with long arms past his greasy black hair to the top shelf. Then all was silent. With the precision of a thief, he lifted the Grand Prize without a sound and set it on the laminate counter top.

"We have a winner!" Mr. Landry called out in the tone of a circus ring leader. "Where is he? Come behind the counter!"

A pair of brothers slithered through. Sissy knew them from around the arcade. They were consistent, those two, and had pooled their tickets. They were nearly the same height, but the older was still a head taller than Sissy. They mounted the stool together, and each placed a hand on the lid and lifted.

"There you are, young lady!" her mother shouted from the doorway. "I expected you home half an hour ago!"

The transfixion of the arcade was temporarily halted; each head turned to the broad lady suffocating the doorway. From the chin up, she had rolled out of bed five minutes ago; her hair was held high like some kind of exotic bird, and her lipstick was a bit smeared. Beneath, she was all business, donning a blouse of white under a waving collar that was a bit too small, like her gray slacks. Even at home and barefoot, she was tall, but here, above thick sandals, she was even more of an imposition.

"Mom, please," Sissy pleaded in a loud whisper, her palms blocking the views of the crowd that seemingly, for the first time, noticed her existence. She slinked closer to her mother. "Those boys just won the Grand Prize. It hardly ever happens!"

"If I'm late to work because of... and your glasses! You'll have to use your old pair in the meantime," she mumbled, dragging her daughter by the sleeve.

Sissy's view of the countertop was completely blocked. The last thing she heard before the glass door closed behind her was the envious "Oh, wow!" typical of a crowd of children.

"How d'ya do, Mrs. Slenderghost?"

The mother and daughter pair turned round and spotted Donnie Finn standing on his hands in the shadows of the arcade, his chicken legs and aging sneakers pinned against the tall windows. Nimbly, he rolled across the pebbled concrete and leaped into a standing position. Donnie's home backed up to the strip mall that housed the arcade, a mere stone's throw away.

Sissy scooted behind her mother.

"We are well, Donald, and it's Mrs. Sindergast. Does your mother know you are here?"

"Oh, sure she does, Mrs. S," he whistled. "She knows I'm somewhere if not at home."

"Well, please be sure to meet her at home on time, do you understand?"

"Yes, ma'am!" Donnie exclaimed. "And hey, Sissy! I see you back there!"

Sissy didn't move a muscle.

"Oh, well, see y'all later!" Donnie hollered as he rolled cartwheels out of sight.

✠

She was sitting on the floor the next morning, criss-cross applesauce, leaning over a gaming magazine. The biceps of animated men ripped their shirt sleeves and hoisted machine guns that rendered an alien species to a puddle of purple muck. Sissy turned the page and heard from the other room, "Goodbye, Sissy, see you at lunchtime!" Moments later, the garage door creaked to a close.

Sissy jumped from the carpet, and as she whipped from room to room, her oversized plaid shirt swished like a cape. Beneath the sofa cushions, she found a quarter, and under the sofa, a nickel. In that one top drawer, she dove beneath pens and paperclips and letters from Father and old grocery lists, making waves of mess all for naught.

Then, it hit her. Again, her mother wasn't home. Her father was in Syria.

She had resisted the temptation a few times before. She shifted towards her parents' bedroom as if her feet had a will and let her mind do the talking, the reasoning. Yes, no, maybe, so she was in there and shut the door as if someone might see her. It was always like this when Father was overseas. A mess, a junkyard, mountains of debris. A large bra was thrown over a bedpost, another was spread like a carcass across the aging carpet. A plastic container overflowing with fourteen years' worth of birthday cards and notes from Father jutted from beneath the dresser. Sissy tiptoed over denim and high-heeled shoes until she reached a pile of purses currently in her mother's rotation crouching in the corner. Sissy blew away the dust bunnies and rummaged through the bags one by one. More letters from father and grocery bills, yes, and a rare dollar bill. She replaced everything as well as she could and crept from the room three dollars richer.

Back on the floor of her room, she spread out the money. After tossing a superfluous nickel and penny into her bottom drawer, she was left with an even seven dollars. She could play Clown

Pound and World's End, both games with safe floors and high ceilings, four times each. Sissy always played Clown Pound as a part of her strategy since the minimum you could earn was always consistently decent; the odds of walking away with anything less than fifteen was very low, and at a cost of a mere fifty cents, it was economical. World's End, on the other hand, was one of a few riskier games that were in Sissy's rotation. When she did well there, she could quadruple what could be earned in just one game of Clown Pound. However, it was even more likely her character would be killed in a matter of seconds, yielding zero tickets, at a cost of fifty cents per game.

She pulled from the bottom drawer her camouflage pencil case overflowing with printed receipts displaying the number of tickets she deposited into the arcade's ticket-counting machine. She had scrimped and saved for almost two full years. Even her thirteenth birthday party was held at the arcade, and instead of presents, she asked for any tickets won by her guests. She unzipped the case, laid out the receipts in descending order, and like she had many dozens of times before, she counted. Sissy had earned 14,254 tickets, just 746 shy of the Grand Prize. Sissy returned everything to its place, pocketed her coins, ignored the pair of old, outdated glasses that her mother had left for her on the kitchen counter, and flew out the front door.

If there were such a thing, it was a cool June day. The sky was a vast cloud with no sun to speak of, and a breeze drew in a hint of chill pulled from storage from months before. It was not a long trek to the arcade, and Sissy had mastered the most efficient route, having walked it countless times. She descended the two stairs of her stoop and turned sharply left across her front yard, meeting the sidewalk at an angle on the far side of her mailbox. She headed north two steps per square, 22, 24, 26, 28, ultimately taking a left on Llewelyn, the road that led from the neighborhood, at 232 steps, give or take.

When she was ten, her father had brought her to the arcade before he was called away for the second time. They had walked this same route. He had grown up in this same neighborhood and shared stories of childhood friends, fun, and many trips to the emergency room for stitches here and there. Up ahead was the ravine past Donnie's house where her father, as a child, lost his balance and fell ten feet, breaking his arm in two places. She glanced in as she passed by.

There was Donnie. He was shirtless and shoeless and crouched, leaning over a puddle of water no deeper than an inch. Even if he himself were not present, evidence that he frequented the ravine—a broken folding chair waiting empty on an island of gray cinderblock, a rotten towel hanging over the edge of the wall, a makeshift cane pole laying prostrate in a puddle—abounded. Beside him sat an old metal pot that looked to be half-filled with dirty water, and he was scooping tadpoles into it as quickly as he could. He glanced up quickly and started yelling.

"Sissy, Sissy! Look what I got here, look! Tadpoles, hundreds of 'em! D'ya wanna see?"

Sissy walked past the ravine faster, pretending like she hadn't heard him or seen him. This wasn't the time for distractions. Today could be her day; but the odds were against her. It would probably be a few more weeks if she could find a way to earn some money, but crazier things have happened, even in that one arcade. Once, a three-year-old threw two quarters into a machine and pressed random buttons before drawing a jackpot of 500 tickets, stolen of course, by her older brother.

There were steps behind her; they were quick and natural, like being chased down by a coyote.

"Sissy! Wait up! Look here!" Donnie darted in front of her path, holding the rusted pot by handles on either end. He stopped abruptly, sloshing a dollop of water and a tadpole or two at Sissy's feet.

"Donnie, I don't have time for this," Sissy declared as she stepped back from the bobbing black tadpole on the sidewalk. Whatever the smell was, whether the water or the boy himself, Sissy bit her tongue, breathing through her mouth. Seeing that she usually avoided him, Sissy had not seen Donnie quite this close for a few months. He was growing taller and thinner, as if stretched taffy could walk and talk.

"That's all right! I'll walk witchya!" As Sissy stepped around him, Donnie took no notice of the slight, bouncing around her like a puppy to the arcade, pestering her with questions. "Where ya going? Why do you spend so much time in there? What's so great about a prize like that anyway? Did you know tomorrow's my birthday? No, Momma's not home a lot and will probably forget." She answered with as few words as possible and, at the door of the arcade, swatted him away.

✠

It was time.

After exchanging loose coins for quarters, Sissy made straight for Clown Pound. She lifted the heavy hammer over the uppermost nine and she placed her left foot next to the hole in the bottom left. *Click, click* the quarters went down the slot, and the clowns came to life. She popped them one after another with her hammer and foot, a flawless beginning. Now two or three, or sometimes four, elusively shot from their holes simultaneously, and each untouched clown darted back in with an irritating chuckle. When the game died with a drawn out clown laugh and a deep breath by Sissy, thirty tickets were spit from the machine, an above-average round. After four rounds, Sissy was 105 tickets closer to her goal.

The quarters grew heavy in her pocket as she waited her turn at World's End, watching another boy launch grenades and ammunition at a never-ending onslaught of zombies and other wicked creatures. He had played three games already, but the longest he could survive was two minutes and twenty seconds. The longer a player lasted in the game, the more tickets he would earn. The rules were simple, but gameplay was very difficult. However, as one of only a few games in the arcade with a healthy sized jackpot, it was worth it.

"Look at all them zombies!" a voice whispered from behind. Sissy clenched her lungs and muscles and turned to see Donnie, who had thrown on a white t-shirt and sandals, staring over her shoulder.

"Donnie, what are you *doing* in here?"

"I'da never played that game, no thanks, too scary. Ooh, look at that thing; look at it! Like a monkey zombie or somethin', no thanks!" As Donnie carried on analyzing each and every scene, his stench tiptoed around the machines. "Oh, oh, shoot it, shoot it! Throw a grenade; look out!" he shouted to the boy playing the game. Gamers of all ages started to stare, peering up from their entertainment and shaking their heads and whispering under their breath.

Sissy grabbed him by the shirt and pulled him straight down. As she pleaded with him to stay out of sight and keep his voice down, he wiped his nose and rubbed his fingers across the floor.

"I gotta right to be here as much as you do," Donnie said as he planted himself on the floor. "'sides, maybe I can be helpful? Maybe if you gave me fifty cents, you know, for my birthday or somethin', I can win you a few tickets?"

"Your birthday's not til tomorrow," she said, scanning around through her one good lens for who may be watching. "Fine, fine, fine," she exhaled on the edge of a solution. "You can hold my quarters for me. And be quiet, for God's sake! Don't make a sound; don't make a scene. But I swear to God, Donnie, if even one quarter goes missing, I'll tell my father, and he's got a gun on him at all times! You understand?"

Donnie gulped and nodded.

✠

One grenade after another, bullets flying, but it was never enough. Zombies, spiders, and all manner of evil crawled from behind overturned cars. Some simply fell from the sky, suspended by web or rope. An earthquake, and sure enough, the crevice Sissy hopped into, what she hoped to be an escape from the terror and blood and hunting was nothing but a dead end. They came. No more grenades. Game over, and with an impressive survival time and near personal best of 4 minutes and 12 seconds, Sissy had earned 80 tickets. Game 2. Enter a building and close the door. This time, two guns, and nonstop repetition of *click, click*

click of bullets flying from the chamber. No time to reload; drop a grenade. Damage taken. Up the stairs? Extra ammo halfway up. At the top, a nasty zombie troll and one swing of his club later, Sissy's character lay lifeless on the second floor. Game time: 3 minutes and 41 seconds. Not bad at all. 70 tickets.

Sissy wheeled around and demanded the final two quarters from Donnie who, as promised, had not said a word. He wanted to, that was obvious, but he bit his lip to near-bleeding to keep it shut.

With a deep breath, Sissy looked up above the machine. A green siren slowly turned above the words JACKPOT: 500 TICKETS, a marquee of hope. The screen before her scrolled the game's tagline: *Can you survive for 5 minutes?* Win the jackpot, win the grand prize. Fall short, and it would be back to begging Mother beneath and through the woman's yelling for more work around the house just to scrimp and save quarters day by day.

"Donnie, quarters!"

Taking the warm quarters from her servant's hand, she slid them down the slot. One chance for the jackpot. One chance for the Grand Prize.

Gun type? Machine gun again. Drop location? The jungle. Begin. The parachute opened up above a sea of green, and the noise of birds chattering through began to rise. As soon as Sissy touched the green treetops, the timer began, and no sooner had she landed, than the evil came, crawling up the trunks of trees. Hopping from treetop to treetop. Nowhere to go; grenade was the only option.

What's that smell? Smells like queer to me!

As the treetops were split open by a flash of light and an ear splitting explosion, Sissy glanced over her shoulder to see two boys on either side of Donnie, both snickering at what they had whispered. That quarter-second distraction was enough time for a damage-taking anaconda strike. No matter. Machine gun fire in circles, down the path. Zombie, zombie, zombie from the treetops, all felled with 3 or 4 bullets. What's that? A temple of some kind. Enter in. A *clink*. What was that? A trigger plate. The entrance closed behind her. A trap door opened. Down the slide, picking up ammo and health along the way...

Fag.

Sissy couldn't look this time, but the shadows on the screen meant a larger crowd, but whether there for her or Donnie, she could not tell. At the bottom of the slide was a dark room. Barrels in the corner, torches on the wall. Within milliseconds, a rumble of the screen and flying sand. Another troll. Not slow and stupid, but rather quick with his flying club. Sissy could halt him for half a second at a time with a few shots to the eyes...

Gollum? Where's your precious?

Sissy felt the tension on the back of her seat from Donnie's hand, almost mounted to her chair, stuck in position by his rigid arm. Jump over the club. Duck under the club. Zombies too!? From the ceiling. Bullets flying, one of which hit the bracket holding the torch. The flame fell to the barrels. *BOOM,* it all exploded. Sand rained like dust blown off an attic trunk onto the lifeless body of the troll. There was a hole in the wall, and Sissy had one half of one heart of health remaining out of ten. The crowd awed and silenced just as quickly. Out of the hole in the wall Sissy ran, zombies behind. *Zip, zip* flew bullets behind, in front, all around. Ten seconds to go.

Bastard.

At this, Sissy turned as the crowd gasped to a hushed silence. Donnie's two-by-four frame stiffened and clenched. By the time she turned back, it was game over. Her character's body lay there as zombies lurked about and snakes slithered through. Four minutes and 56 seconds. She had earned 90 tickets, 401 shy of her goal of 15,000 to earn the Grand Prize.

Bastard. Bastard. Bastard. It was a chorus of whispers. Mr. Landry, who watched with a careful eye from the prize counter, surely could not hear what was being said. Sissy met Donnie's eyes. He wanted to punch but had promised her.

"You don't know me," Donnie said to the fattest of the boys. "You don't know nothin' 'bout me."

"I don't have to," replied the fat one. "One *look* at you is plenty."

"All right, boys, stand aside! Routine maintenance! Excuse me!" The screen went black. Mr. Landry had unplugged the game and stood over them all with a toolbox in one hand. The jingle of hammers and wrenches lightened the air.

"I think my work here is done, Sissy. Sorry 'bout your game." Donnie pushed his way through the crowd and out the glass doors.

✠

Sissy was a ghost from one of the games. No coins remaining and no hope of acquiring new ones for who knows how long. She wandered machine to machine, hovering about the boys lost in other worlds, watching through one lens as they pocketed handfuls of tickets. The Grand Prize loomed over them; it was heaven. She was a specter in a perpetual purgatory. The box the prize had been placed in this time was larger than usual. Sissy thought, by the looks of it, it must be a bit heavy.

The clock on the wall said that her mother would be home soon, and if Sissy wasn't there to meet her, it meant more yelling. More yelling. More and more yelling. Always when Father wasn't home. It clung to the walls and slipped in under the covers, echoing from room to room, a pinball machine.

Sissy turned to the door and saw through her cracked lens the fat boy slip something of an odd color into the ticket machine. Whatever it was, it was white, not red like the 240 tickets bulging from her own pocket. Cooly, she slipped around the arcade and at a good angle, she approached the machine unnoticed and silent. She peered over.

The boy did it again, then again. Strips of paper cut to the shape of tickets, in rows of three or four, one after another. These weren't arcade tickets but an imitation.

Sissy cleared her throat, "Ahem."

"Oh, what? Yeah, sure, go right ahead, you go, you go first," the fat one stammered.

Sissy stepped to the machine and began inserting her streams of tickets, sucked in at a rapid rate. The sound was satisfying, *tick tick tick tick*, like a clock wound to run at high speed. The fat boy was not entranced. He rocked on his heels and wiped his brow, all while staring at the ceiling from whence no noise came and where there were no flashing lights.

"What were you doing just now?" Sissy asked.

"Shut up and mind your own, girl!" the fat one said.

"Oh, Mr. Landry!" Sissy spoke in a soft but high-pitched tone.

"All right, all right, shut up!" The fat boy insisted. He let out a breath. "They're fake." With his chubby fingers, he reached into the deep pockets of his cargo shorts and pulled out a single strip. It was paper but a bit thicker, like the paper her father's letters came home written on. Sissy rubbed her fingers across the ridges, roughly cut into the same shape as those of the red ones from the machines. At the barrier where two tickets were to meet, the fat boy had creased it by bending them back and forth and back and forth to mimic the true, perforated bond. All things considered, it was, besides the color, a well-done imitation. That is, as long as Mr. Landry didn't find out.

"But isn't that stealing from the arcade? From Mr. Landry?"

"Ah, shut up, Ms. Perfect. If he didn't have plenty of money, there wouldn't even be a Grand Prize. Besides, it's not just me doing it. How do you think the Marcus brothers did it? You really think anyone can save up enough tickets to actually win?"

He had a point; it *was* almost impossible. Why create a prize that no one could win? Her mother always said she had to snatch and claw and fight to get what she had. Her father was in Syria. He was aggressive, he was bold. He carried a gun and hunted the real bad guys. There were no real bad guys here. She had done enough, paid who knows how many hundreds of dollars into these machines and for what? To fall nearly 500 tickets shy of the Grand Prize. Whatever was in that box was something big, something amazing, something heavy, the envy of all in the arcade. And, who knows? Who's to say there would be another Grand Prize after this one was earned? Sissy had an advantage: she already had worked to earn over the last two years more than 14,500 real, red tickets, with the receipts to prove it.

"Good luck," Sissy said as she ripped her receipt from the machine. She walked away, the fat boy's small strip of imitation tickets now in her pocket.

✠

The next morning was a gray one. The humidity that each previous day had enveloped her in immediate sweat had parted. Though clouds crept in, hinting at a soon-to-be shower, each step on the concrete sidewalk was crisp; her heels crackled against the rough cement as she walked.

The previous evening, it had taken her hours and hours, much longer than she anticipated. It wasn't mistakes that cost her, though she had made her fair share in the first half hour of work. It was the sheer monotony, the repetition, the detail; it was the curves and ridges of each of the tickets. Around 7:30, she ran out of card stock, so father's letters were the next to go, then even the baseball cards in her bottom drawer. When they were gone, that's when the danger started. Fortunately for her, mother went to bed early. Slowly, so slowly, she pushed open the door to her mother's bedroom and crawled like father had taught her to the plastic container of years of birthday cards under the dresser. The old digital clock on the bedside table showed 9:44 PM and haunted the room in a stale red glare. Sissy had to repeat this step three times over an hour.

She sped past Donnie's house, and a good thing too. The shirtless boy was sitting in the backyard grass, a large glass jar at his side, facing away from the road. Once or twice, he jabbed with his quick hand into the yard and dropped whatever he was able to grab in the makeshift environment. Thankfully unseen, she sped around the edge of the strip mall and into the arcade, which was active for only having been open for less than half an hour. A sliver of Mr. Landry flashed through the small pane of glass on his office door. He was pacing back and forth on the phone, which was tethered to the wall by a curly black cord. This was Sissy's first chance.

She started with the fat boy's fake tickets from the day before so that, if caught, someone could share in her blame.

It worked.

Now three of her own.

Tick tick tick.

Three more, and three more, and four more, and three more. Her heart raced, the blood flowed; it was nerve wracking; it was exciting; but most of all it was working. After three minutes that felt like thirty, she punched RECEIPT. The deed was halfway done.

Sissy wandered penniless about the arcade. One lucky boy earned a small jackpot of fifty tickets by stopping a flashing light on the right bulb. Another boy tested his skill at World's End, which Sissy had nearly conquered the previous day. Lasting only a minute or more, the boy flew through his quarters two at a time until they were all expended. He, like her, began to wander, though, unlike her, he shared in the arcade's revelry. She hated his smile, despised the colored lights refracting in his eyes.

This was Sissy's time, time to finish the deal. With a glance left and right, she approached the ticket reader and began again. *Tick tick tick.* Again. *Tick tick.* The letters from Father were all in, as well as a few baseball cards. Fifty tickets left in her pocket. Forty. Thirty. Twenty. *Tick tick tick tick tick tick tiiiiiiiickkkkk.*

The machine was stuck, jammed. It clicked *tick tick* on repeat but couldn't register the tickets. Sissy tried to remove the ticket, but it was in too deep. She circled the machine, shaking it a bit, and the boys began to stare. She caught the glance of the fat boy from the previous day, who shivered with nerves that the scheme may be brought to light. Some other boys began to murmur. She leaned over and desperately peered into the slot, closing one eye, then another, back and forth to focus the image, but it was darkness.

"What's the matter, my girl?"

Sissy looked up and went pale. Mr. Landry towered over her with his ostrich neck. She had never seen him this close before. There was no stench about him, as was rumored, but one eye did appear larger than the other, obvious to see through his thick frames. With his left arm, he clutched a large, overflowing notebook to his chest.

"Unsure, huh? Well, don't worry; this happens all the time!" He bent down and inspected the slot where the tickets could be inserted and, like Sissy had done, circled the machine. He reached down with outstretched fingers and turned the machine on and off. *Tick,* the stuck ticket was sucked in, and Sissy's current ticket count remained on the screen.

Sissy craned her neck upwards from the now working machine into the gaze of Mr. Landry. It took work, like a mountain climb with the eyes. Behind the man, the flickering, almost noisy glare of a dying fluorescent light burned the edges of his face.

"Good as new," he declared, and he disappeared into the office.

✠

Back at home, and after lunch with her mother and the completion of too many unpaid chores, she counted the receipts. Twice, three times, counted. 15,012 was the total of the numbers printed on the paper slips, just above the 15,000 required for the Grand Prize. The clock struck 3:45. Her mother would not be home again until 5:15. Her time had come.

Her steps were heavy, and as the soft rain fell on her clothing and shoes, the trek became more difficult. Seeing the possibility of this, Sissy had put all the receipts in a sandwich bag, then folded that bag into another sandwich bag, then put that bag in her pocket. All the more, the walk was a drag.

"Sissy!"

Through her broken lens, she peered down upon him in the ravine.

"Sissy, get down here! I think I saw a snake crawl under this bridge!"

"Sorry, Donnie, no time," she squealed, quickening her step.

His pleas bounded alongside her and clung to her shoulder until she finally rounded the corner of the strip mall for the second time that day. Here it is. Glory, fame, gift, popularity. What would all those boys say? All those boys who belittled her. All those boys who didn't give her a second look or any kind of a chance. Better yet, what would her mother say? Could she even tell her mother? Would the gift be taken from her? Better write to Father first for his advice. This thinking filled her mind to the brim until she pulled with a heave on the heavy glass doors of the arcade.

Locked.

She tried the other door. Locked. The "emergency exit only" backdoor that kids routinely went in and out of? Locked. The front door, again. Locked. Why? Why was it locked? This was not fair, not fair! To her left was an empty parking lot, to her right, a group of the boys usually in the arcade at this time loitered in front of a used electronics store far, far down the strip mall. How could this be? What was going on? Sissy put her face to the glass on the right side of the arcade. The machines, always dancing with life, exploding with lights and colors and sounds, were unplugged or turned off. The laughter of kids her age, the shouts of joy, gasps of hope and excitement, were all dead. She came to the door one last time, still locked, removed her glasses, and put her face as close as she could against the warm glass.

Sissy jumped and screamed as the other glass door was thrust open. There towered Mr. Landry, just as above the ticket machine, with the overflowing notebook pinned to his chest by his left arm.

"Oh, Sissy!" he let out through a loud laugh. "I saw you looking through from my office door, so I came to open it up! How can I help you on this rainy afternoon?"

"I, uh," she stammered, "I, um, I came to get the Grand Prize." And at that moment, Sissy reached deep into her wet denim pockets and pulled out the bag of receipts.

Mr. Landry took the receipts and, with amazing speed, added up the total one by one, murmuring numbers slower than his mind could work. "You're right, Sissy! 15,012 tickets, what an accomplishment!" He turned back inside, letting the foggy door close with a soft squeak as he retrieved the Grand Prize from the top shelf.

Sissy could tell it was not as heavy as she had thought. This was confirmed when the white box, held together neatly with flowing red ribbon, was rested in her arms.

"But, Mr. Landry," Sissy interjected, slouching over the gift with a hunched posture, "what is going on with the arcade?"

"Well, you see, kiddo, we're closing down. Was just about to hang the CLOSED sign on the window for good. We've had a good run, but it just wasn't enough to make ends meet." Then, seeing the shock and sadness in her eyes, he continued. "And don't you worry about me! I've got more work lined up."

If Sissy had been a ghost here the day before, now she was frozen in time, a statue on the spot. The Grand Prize felt heavy now, heavier than her clothes, heavier than her footsteps, a box of bricks pressing down with awful force on her forearms and palms.

"I," she began, "I," she wobbled, "I," she whispered to fill the gaps in thought, "I can't accept this." And at that, she lifted the box back to the man.

"Oh, sure you can, kiddo," Mr. Landry insisted, outstretching his right arm to resist the return. "It's got your name on it."

Glancing down, there it was, only a corner sticking out from under the patch of ribbon on the top. Sissy couldn't spare the hand, so Mr. Landry himself reached down with the gentle fingers of his right hand to move the bow out of the way. Taped there on top of the box was a ticket she had made from the letters of her father, and etched across this particular name was a signature which, though it had cut off the first name, clearly read in messy ink: *Sindergast.*

"Now, Cecilia," the man whispered, hardly audible over the building sobs of the girl. He slowly fell to one knee. She could hardly make him out, but as he wiped the tears with his handkerchief, the vision of him became clearer. They were face to face, almost eyelash to eyelash. She went back and forth, the small eye to the big eye, the big eye to the small eye, not knowing exactly where to rest her gaze.

"Now, Cecilia," he whispered again. "I have known your father for over thirty years. This," he emphasized as he tapped on the box, "is not who you are. Now," he said as he straightened up, "this prize is yours, but I think you know exactly what to do with it."

At last her eyes squared perfectly with his. At first, Sissy had no idea. She could not get the image of being handcuffed by her own father and thrown into the back of a Humvee out of her mind, her mother in the seat next to her, shouting threats and insults. What would her father say if he ever found out? What would her mother do? Oh, the yelling! The yelling! Her father would come home soon, then the yelling at each other.

That's how it always was when Father returned. First a makeup, then, less than a week later, the yelling came back. No, anything but that. Anything at all. Then, like the soft, first light of dawn, it came to her. Yes, she knew exactly what to do with the Grand Prize.

"Go," he said, seeing the realization wipe across her face. So, she nodded and went. First, left, away from the doors of the now-closed arcade. Then, wrap around the building at the edge of the strip mall. Over the bridge, first house on the right.

About the Author

Philip J Martin is a graduate of both Auburn University and Franciscan University of Steubenville. In 2014 he was awarded Second Prize in the Tuscany Prize in Catholic Fiction, and in 2015 he was awarded First Prize in the same competition. His writing was essential in the making of the documentary film *Sign of Contradiction*, and he both edited and contributed to the accompanying anthology of the same name, both by 4PM Media. His fiction stories, poetry, and nonfiction boast numerous publications both online and in print. Philip lives in and writes from beautiful Daphne, AL and enjoys spending his free time with his wife and children.

Full Quiver Publishing
PO Box 244
Pakenham, ON K0A2X0
Canada
www.fullquiverpublishing.com